SAVAGE GROUNDS
A DALTON SAVAGE MYSTERY
BOOK 1

L.T. RYAN

WITH
BIBA PEARCE

Copyright © 2022 by L.T. Ryan, Biba Pearce, Brian Christopher Shea, & Liquid Mind Media. All rights reserved. No part of this publication may be copied, reproduced in any format, by any means, electronic or otherwise, without prior consent from the copyright owner and publisher of this book. This is a work of fiction. All characters, names, places and events are the product of the author's imagination or used fictitiously. For information contact:

contact@ltryan.com

http://LTRyan.com

https://www.facebook.com/groups/1727449564174357

ONE

HE FELT SO ALIVE. The fresh air, the exertion, the early morning sun on his back. There's nothing like it, Mark thought, as he walked along the rugged trail, his boots crunching over the loose ground. To top it all, it was a beautiful spring day, the sky a cobalt blue above the stabbing mountain peaks.

The path meandered around a haphazard pile of boulders that had tumbled down a millennium ago. It then split into two trails. Mark veered left, climbing the steep elevation for—according to the map—six hundred and twenty-three yards. He wondered if someone had actually counted them. He felt the burn in his calves, but kept going, loving every minute of it.

Panting, he reached the top of the slope where the trail flattened out. Wow, the view was something else. He could see for miles. The smudge of a town below started to wake, roused by the honeyed sunshine creeping over the valley. Using his phone camera, he shot a short video of the panorama.

An eagle soared past, riding an air current. Mark took a deep, satisfying breath. He was on top of the world. Up here, he didn't have to answer to anyone. The pressing deadlines of his job at the tourism company faded in relation to the stacked boulders, tall trees, and endless vistas. His sister's divorce, his father's upcoming surgery, and his own disillusionment with life paled in comparison to this vastness.

Then there was her.

Her.

The woman with no name. A fleeting encounter on a deserted mountain trail. He smiled at the memory. Wild hair, nymph-like features, eyes you could lose yourself in. Would he see her again? He hoped so. Out here, where time was measured in falling leaves and flowing streams, anything was possible.

A worn signpost ahead pointed toward Stony Ridge, ten miles down the trail and his final destination. He took the creased map out of his back pocket and studied the route. The cell phone reception was sporadic up here. He'd had time to post one picture before he reached the lookout point. Now he was out of range.

Using the map meant old schooling it, but that was fine with him. In fact, he preferred it that way. It felt more authentic. As long as his phone camera worked, that was all he cared about. He could document the trail and post it on the website later.

A lizard scampered across the path in front of him. A flash of silver in his peripheral vision, then it was gone, swallowed by the underbrush.

He refocused on the map. Ahead, he noticed a thick, forested area intersected by steady streams and shallow creeks. The map showed a spiderweb of tiny blue lines weaving through the green. Fun.

Pocketing the map, he took one last look at the view, then set off along the trail.

The forest had its own appeal. Majestic pines and aspens filtered the sunlight, casting dappled pools on the uneven ground. Each side of the path bulged with underground roots and wildflowers, and berry bushes licked his ankles as he walked.

Mark sighed at the welcome drop in temperature. The perspiration on his skin cooled, and he gave an involuntary shiver. A squirrel scampered up a tree in front of him, and he paused to watch it leap from bough to bough before it disappeared.

Some hikers liked to listen to music, but he preferred the sounds of the trail. The birds chirping overhead, small animals scurrying over fallen leaves, insects buzzing, water trickling.

A dampness sat in the air, and sure enough, he rounded the next bend and came to a gushing creek. A fallen log had been positioned over it, supported by stones on either side. He clambered onto it, feeling it wobble beneath his weight. The next minute, he was sitting on his ass waist deep in the water.

Idiot.

He should have seen that coming. Usually, he was pretty solid on his feet. He stood and waded to the other side. The water gurgled around his ankles as he felt the tug of the current.

Reaching for his phone, he checked to see it was still dry. Yes, it was working. Thank goodness for that. It meant his photos were intact. The same couldn't be said for the drenched map in his back pocket. He took it out, but it fell apart in his hands. Useless.

Sighing, he scrunched it into a ball and stuffed it in the waterproof section of his pack. This would make things interesting. He'd have to rely on signposts and trailheads to get to the ridge now. These mountains were crisscrossed with trails, so it wouldn't be easy.

He continued for another mile, pausing only to take photographs and the occasional sip from his water bottle. His wet shorts chafed his thighs, but they'd dry as soon as he got back into the sun.

The trail narrowed as it wound through more dense forest. Trees and bushes curled around the barely visible track, enveloping him. Taking out his phone, he filmed his progress. Viewers loved feeling like they were right there on the trail with you.

He was approaching another, thankfully smaller creek when a shadowy figure emerged from the trees. It was unexpected, but not uncommon to meet other hikers around these parts. The Stony Ridge trail was tough for a recreational hiker—it scored an arduous eight out of ten on his website's rating system—so he studied the approaching man with interest.

"Howdee." He stopped filming and pocketed his phone.

"Hey, how ya doing?" The man had a deep, baritone voice and Mark could tell he was used to the outdoors. It wasn't just the man's deep tan or rugged physique, but more the casual stance, the ease with which he moved along. This man was comfortable here.

Like him.

Except where Mark was slim and geeky looking, this guy was handsome and athletic. He reminded Mark of the jocks he used to avoid in high school.

Hey four-eyes, you unplug yourself from your laptop yet?

"I'm good, how about you?"

He wasn't that person anymore, especially not out here on the trail. Out here he was *Overlord*, anti-hero, and warrior. The trail name had been given to him by the guys he worked with on account of a video game he used to play, and the fact that nobody rated and reviewed as many hikes as he did.

"Good. You heading up to Stony Ridge?" the man asked.

"Yeah, that's the plan," Mark replied.

"Awesome. It's a good day for it."

Mark nodded. The man was blocking the path, so he had to wait for him to pass before moving on.

"I'm Walker." The jock held out a beefy hand.

"As in Texas Ranger?" Mark joked, although the man could be, given his size and build.

Walker laughed. "No way. I'm the furthest thing from it."

Mark smiled. "They call me Overlord."

A knowing grin. "Good to meet ya. Looks like you had a fall there?" He eyed the wet shorts.

"Yeah, lost my footing in the creek."

"Bummer. Easy thing to happen."

Walker was being kind. Seasoned hikers knew to test a log before they stepped on it. Mark hadn't been paying attention. "You been up to the ridge?"

"Yeah, I've been on the trail a few days now." Walker spread his arms. "Time to head back to civilization."

The path back down was easy enough. "You don't have an extra map on you, by any chance?" Mark inquired. "Mine disintegrated on account of the creek."

The hiker snorted. "Probably. Let me take a look."

He slipped off his backpack and set it on the ground. Strange that he didn't have a map on hand if he'd been rambling for days. Still, he could be familiar with the trail.

"You come up here often?" Mark asked.

"Nah, first time. I move around a lot." The hiker rummaged in the backpack. A shock of pink caught Mark's eye, and he noticed a small, fluffy pendant hanging from the zipper. It was an odd token for a buff guy like Walker.

"Ah, here it is." He pulled out the map and handed it over. "Thought I had one."

"You don't need it?"

"Nah, not anymore. Heading downhill ain't hard."

Fair enough. Still, the map looked new and unused without a crinkle on it. Mark frowned. How'd the guy get up here without a map?

"You got kids?" Mark glanced at the stuffed toy.

"No, why'd you ask?" Then he noticed where Mark was looking. "That's my niece's. She gave it to me for my birthday. It's my good luck charm."

It was the way he said it, a tad too quick. Mark hesitated. Something wasn't right, but he couldn't put his finger on it. Time to move on. "I'd better be on my way if I want to make it before sunset."

"Sure, nice talking to you," Walker said.

"Thanks again for the map." Mark held it up.

"No problem."

They passed each other, chest to chest. The stranger was much broader than him and Mark was forced to take a step backwards off the path into the underbrush. He cringed as a thorn bush dug into his thigh. They passed each other with a final nod and Mark continued on his way.

After the smaller creek, the trail closed in on itself. Prickly branches reached out in front of him, creating a natural barrier. He swept them aside, careful not to scratch himself. It was impossible to see more than a few feet ahead, but this was the most overgrown section of the hike. In a few hundred yards, the trees would open up and he'd be back on the winding, dusty trail up to the ridge.

That's how he remembered it, anyway. Maybe he ought to check. He unfolded the map the stranger had given him and peered down. A rustling behind him made him pause. This was bear territory. Heart pounding, he turned around.

Slowly.

Don't make any sudden moves.

A hard object whacked the side of his head. His skull exploded with pain, and his vision blacked out.

The next thing he remembered was the feel of the mossy footpath under his cheek and the sensation of being dragged off the trail, through the underbrush.

TWO

HAWK'S LANDING COUNTY SHERIFF DALTON SAVAGE sat opposite his fiancé, Becca, and cradled a cup of coffee. It was his second of the day, but then this was a two-cup discussion. Becca was sipping herbal tea. At five-months pregnant, she was watching what she ate and drank.

"Should we set a date?"

Her face softened. "There's no rush, is there?"

His gaze fell to the baby bump just starting to show. "I wouldn't say that, exactly."

She laughed. "You know I don't want a big wedding, Dalton." Becca didn't have any family to speak of. Both her parents had died several years back, and she never spoke about them. Savage got the impression they weren't close.

"Sure, that works." He wasn't a fan of big weddings either, although there were a few people he wanted to invite. Jasmine, for one. He thought of her as a second mother, and even though his relationship with her daughter, Rachel Hatch, had never amounted to anything, they still were close. Then there was Barbara Wright at the station. The admin secretary was mother hen to him and his colleagues. He'd never hear the end of it if he didn't invite her to the ceremony.

"We could elope?" Becca said.

Savage hesitated, trying to read her clear blue gaze. "Really?"

"Why not? I like the thought of it just being you and me."

It was appealing. "We'll need a couple of witnesses," he pointed out.

She sighed and stroked her belly. It was crazy to think there was an unborn child in there, growing bigger every day. *His* child. "I know. Well, how about a Justice of the Peace wedding? We could have a small reception afterwards, just close friends."

He noted she didn't say family. "Sounds great," he said.

The pregnancy had taken them both by surprise. They'd only been dating a few months when they'd found out, though it didn't change their trajectory. If anything, it confirmed what he'd been thinking. For the first time in his life, Savage felt a sense of calm. Becca was good for him. He liked to think the reverse was true, too. When she looked at him in a certain way, he felt her love. And it felt right, so he'd proposed. It had been a little cheesy, but she hadn't said no. That was something.

Savage smiled at the memory.

"What are you thinking?" Becca asked, her voice soft.

"Nothing."

"You know I can read you like a book." She raised an eyebrow.

He chuckled. "I was thinking about how you almost ate the engagement ring."

She threw back her head and laughed. "You're the idiot that put it in the pancake mix. How was I supposed to know?"

He shrugged. "It seemed like a good idea at the time."

Becca got up and came around the table, then bent over to kiss him. "Crazy man. I love you, you know that?"

He nodded. "I love you too."

And he did.

A year ago, he wouldn't have thought it possible, but now... The one person he couldn't risk losing was Becca.

The phone rang, distracting him from Becca's embrace.

He glanced at the screen. It was Barbara at the Hawk's Landing Sheriff's office. "I'd better get that."

Becca nodded and went back to her herbal tea.

"Hi Barbara, what's up?"

"Good day to you too, mister," came her tart reply.

He grinned. "Sorry. How are you doing?"

"I'm good. I just called to let you know Jesse Turner was released on parole."

Savage paused. "He was?"

"Yeah, four days ago. We just heard."

Hell, that was soon. Just a couple of years back, Savage's predecessor had put him away for robbing a convenience store and assaulting an elderly customer. "How come he's out so early?"

"Overcrowding. They gave early parole to everyone with under a year left on their sentence."

He shook his head. Unbelievable. "Who's his parole officer?"

A few clicks of her computer mouse. "It doesn't say."

He'd have to find out. That boy was trouble with a capital T. Wouldn't be long before he'd offend again.

"According to the report, he's wearing an ankle bracelet and can't leave the county. Those were the conditions of his early parole."

Like that'll hold him.

"Thanks for letting me know. Anything else?"

"Yeah, we've got a missing person case. Thorpe's already on it."

"He is?" Savage got up off the chair, scraping it on the kitchen floor. Becca glanced up from her newspaper.

"What?" she mouthed.

"Missing person," he told her, covering the phone with his hand.

She frowned and gave a small nod.

"I'll be in soon." Savage hung up and turned to Becca. "Gotta go." He wanted to get to the office, but there was something he had to take care of first.

"Sure. See you later. Don't forget the scan at five."

"I won't."

He kissed her goodbye, then grabbed his keys and his sheriff's badge off the countertop and strode out the door.

. . .

SAVAGE DROVE his Chevy Suburban up the winding driveway to Jasmine's house. On the radio, a news reporter talked about a daring heist at a bank in Durango. Broad daylight. No fatalities. Five hundred thousand dollars stolen. The perps had shot out the security cameras on entry, terrifying the customers. "Anyone with information should contact the Durango Sheriff's office on—Turning off the radio, he thought about his task. He'd been meaning to speak to Jasmine for a while now and couldn't put it off any longer. Not with the wedding on the horizon.

As he switched off the engine, the front door opened, and Jed Russell walked out. The retired Army veteran who'd saved Hatch's life stood on the porch and watched as Savage got out of his SUV.

"Mornin' Sheriff." He tipped his hat. Two kids ran out beside him. The first thought that struck Savage was how much Daphne had grown. She was almost as tall as her older brother. Perhaps she took after her Aunt Rachel who was 5'10". Jake—less boisterous than his sister—stood by Jed's side, a smile on his handsome face.

"Hey Mr. Savage," Jake said, pleased to see him.

Savage was hit by a pang of guilt. He hadn't been down this way in a while.

"How are you, Jake?" Savage ruffled the boy's hair before shaking hands with the older man. "Jed."

"I'm good. You here to see grandma?" Jake asked.

Savage nodded. "Yeah. Is she in?"

The smell of roasted coffee beans drifted out of the door toward him.

"Never mind," he said. "I know that smell. There's only one person in the world who makes coffee that good."

Jed grinned and stepped aside to let him enter. "You know the way."

He did. The first time he'd come here was when he'd started investigating Jasmine's eldest daughter's murder. Hatch couldn't sit by while her sister's killer was still out there. A retired military cop, she'd begun her own investigation. That's how they'd met. He'd quickly realized that the best way to handle Hatch was to work with her, not against her. That's how their relationship had started.

It was important to him that Jasmine was on board with him marrying Becca. For some inexplicable reason, he needed her to be okay with it.

"Hey stranger." She gave him a warm hug. "Long time, no see."

"I know. I'm sorry I haven't been around lately."

She waved his apology away. "Don't be. Life gets in the way, I know that. Can I get you a cup?" She gestured to the percolator.

He grinned. "You know I won't say no."

She filled a cup and handed it to him. "So, what brings you out here?"

"How's Hatch?"

Jasmine shrugged, a sadness creeping into her gaze. "You know my daughter. Same as always."

"Heard from her lately?"

"No. Don't expect to, either."

Savage nodded.

"Is that why you came?" she asked.

"Not really." He smiled. Jasmine knew him almost as well as Becca did. "I wanted to talk to you about Becca."

"Becca?" Her teal eyes widened. "Why me? Is something wrong?"

"No, not at all." He hesitated. How could he put this? Best just to come right out with it. "I've asked her to marry me."

Jasmine gazed at him for a long moment, then broke into a sad smile. "I'm happy for you, Savage."

"Really?" His eyes narrowed. Did she mean it, or was she just saying that? "I wanted you to be the first to know. We haven't announced it yet."

"It's only right, what with the baby coming."

He nodded. In a small town like this, everyone knew everybody's business.

She sighed. "You know I love my daughter, but I'm the first to admit how stubborn she can be."

Stubborn was an understatement.

"I know she missed her chance with you." Jasmine shook her head, her silver mane falling over one shoulder. "Now she's got to make her own way. Your way is here with Becca and the baby. You have a family to think about now."

He watched her, saying nothing.

Her eyes crinkled. "You deserve to be happy. I know Rachel would want that for you."

He broke into a relieved smile. "Thanks, Jasmine. It means a lot."

She reached over and patted his hand. "Don't mention it. Now drink up, I'm sure you've got a busy day ahead."

That he did.

"Missing person," he admitted.

She cocked her head. "In that case, I'll get you a thermos to go."

He hugged her, taking the flask of her special brew. "You're the best."

"Don't be silly. You'd better be on your way." Her face clouded, and he knew she was thinking back to her other daughter's disappearance. "Every missing person counts. You know that."

He nodded gravely. "All too well."

THREE

SAVAGE WALKED into the small lobby at the sheriff's office and waved at Barbara, who immediately poked her head out from behind a filing cabinet. "Here are the details on Jesse Turner's parole." She handed him a manilla folder.

"Thanks." He knew the case well, having arrived at Hawk's Landing in time for Jesse's arraignment. It was Savage's predecessor who'd arrested the man, though.

A thick plexiglass separated the lobby from the inner workings of the office. Through it, he could see Thorpe and Littleton sitting at their desks. Sinclair wasn't in yet, but she often performed community visits on her way to the office.

After swiping his fob against the gray wall pad to gain entry, he pushed open the door. A short corridor widened into an office space with a cluster of desks in the center. Thorpe, seated closest to the entrance, glanced up.

"Morning." He was jotting down information from his computer screen onto a notepad in front of him.

James Thorpe, a Tennessee native, was Hawk's Landing's newest deputy. As usual, his desk was meticulously tidy, the case files placed in a neat pile to one side, his computer in the middle, and a canister of pencils on the other, all sharpened.

"Morning." Savage stopped by his desk. "Tell me about this missing person."

Thorpe nudged his glasses up his nose. "Her name is Candice Ray, twenty-two years old, lives at the Hidden Gem trailer park. That's—" He glanced down at his notes.

"On the edge of town," Savage finished. "I know it."

Thorpe nodded. "Her mother reported her missing this morning."

Savage had dealt with the trailer park before and wasn't looking forward to paying the residents another visit.

"Okay, let's go talk to her." He spun on his heel as he traced his hand along his hip to check his service firearm.

"What should I do, boss?" asked Littleton, swiveling in his chair. The youngest deputy in the department, he was still learning the ropes, although he'd grown in the last few months. Because they were such a small department, the rookie had experienced a sharp learning curve. Usually, he'd be assigned a Field Training Officer to mentor him and teach him the ropes. Here, he was learning on the job.

"See what you can dig up on Candy Ray," he said. "Her name rings a bell."

"Okay." The thin deputy turned back to his computer.

Thorpe hurried to his feet, grabbing his silver star out of the desk drawer and clipping it to his pocket. After checking his holster, he followed Savage, running to keep up.

THE TRAILER PARK hadn't changed much since the last time he was here. Chaotic rows of double wide trailers and mobile homes sprawled amongst the pines. Dirty awnings, wooden porches, and drooping clotheslines characterized the exteriors, while the unkempt yards were filled with an assortment of tires, furniture, and other household objects in various states of disrepair.

A man sat on a plastic chair whittling a block of wood, his suspicious eyes following the Suburban as it inched along the road to Candice Ray's mother's house.

The welcome hadn't changed either.

"I get the feeling we're not wanted," Thorpe muttered.

"You're right about that." Savage squinted as he studied the numbers on the units. Forty-three, forty-four. According to the missing person's report, Mrs. Ray lived at fifty-two. "There's no love lost between them and us."

"Why's that?"

"Long story. Let's just say the previous sheriff did nothing for the community here."

Thorpe nodded.

"That must be it." Savage pointed to a dilapidated home with grimy windows and weeds in the front yard. On the siding of the mobile home, a wooden number five hung askew, and the two had fallen off completely, but the house was positioned between fifty-one and fifty-three, so it must be the right place.

They parked in the overgrown driveway and walked to the door, past a dopey garden gnome and a rusty old bicycle. Somewhere beyond the trees, Savage could hear the hollow echo of wind chimes.

Next to him, Thorpe shivered. "They always sound spooky to me."

The door opened before they could knock. A woman in her mid-forties stood there, holding a cigarette. Smoke seeped out of the trailer behind her.

"Mrs. Ray?" Savage inquired.

Her gaze narrowed. "You from the sheriff's office?"

"Yes, ma'am. I'm Sheriff Savage and this is Deputy Thorpe. We've come to talk to you about your daughter, Candice. You reported her missing?"

He noticed her hands were shaking. The red butt of the cigarette bobbed about like a firefly. "Yeah, she's been gone a couple of days now. It's not like her. I was getting worried."

Savage squinted behind her into the smoky interior and thought he saw a man lying on the sofa. "That your husband?" he asked.

"No." She stepped out and shut the door. "That's nobody."

Savage frowned. He'd need a name, but it could wait. "Let's talk about Candice."

She took another drag. The firefly grew bright, suspended in space, then began bobbing about again.

"When did you last see your daughter, Mrs. Ray?"

"Martha. I saw her the day before yesterday. She came over before work, but I haven't seen or heard from her since."

"You try calling her?" It was an obvious question, but one he had to ask.

"Yeah, goes straight to voicemail." She gave Savage a pointed look. "Candy never turns her phone off."

Alarm bells started ringing. Still, he didn't want to jump to conclusions.

"Okay, where does your daughter work?" Savage inquired. Thorpe was taking notes, scribbling on his pad in his neat, slanted handwriting.

"At the Roadhouse. That's a bar five miles out of town."

"I know it." Not that he'd had much reason to visit it. It was a rowdy bar, frequented by bikers and local residents. Occasionally, the fights got out of hand. He'd heard stories, but they hadn't had to send anyone out since he'd become sheriff. The man inside gave a muffled cough.

"Is it normal for her to stay out overnight?"

"Yeah, she has a room above the bar, but she checks in every few days, brings me groceries and the like." Her voice rose an octave. "I'm nearly out of booze and cigarettes." The woman seemed more upset about that than the fact her daughter was missing.

"If you don't mind me asking, Martha, why did you wait three days to report your daughter missing?"

She sucked on her cigarette, burning it right down to the filter. "I just figured she must be busy." Smoke curled out of the sides of her mouth as she spoke. Shooting the butt a disgusted look, she dropped it onto the grass and stamped it underfoot. It joined multiple others on the ground.

"Does Candice have a boyfriend?" Savage asked.

"No one serious. She hasn't been involved with anyone since

Jesse." She reached into her pocket for the box of cigarettes and took another out. Her fingers were stained yellow, her nails bitten to the quick.

Jesse? Had he heard correctly?

"Jesse Turner?"

"Yeah. You know him?"

Savage cleared his throat. "You could say that."

She lit up another cigarette, breathing in deeply. "Then you know she ratted him out? He went to jail because of her." A plume of smoke shot into the air as she exhaled.

It was prison, actually, but he didn't correct her. Her nose crinkled as if she'd smelled something bad. It was unclear if it was Jesse that she found unpalatable, or the fact her daughter had ratted him out.

Savage *knew* he'd heard her name before. Candy Ray had been Jesse Turner's girlfriend, the one who'd testified against him in court. She was the sole reason he'd been put away.

Thorpe's forehead wrinkled as he connected the dots. "Jesse Turner was released four days ago," he said quietly.

She looked indignant. "I heard."

"You haven't seen him since then?" Savage asked. "He hasn't been around here?"

"No way. After those letters he sent Candy, he ain't welcome around here. We'd have seen him off if he'd come anywhere near the place."

Savage frowned. "What letters?"

Thorpe paused, pen in the air.

"Those letters he wrote her from jail. He said some terrible things, like how he blamed her for putting him away, and how he was going to get even when he got out."

"He threatened her?" Savage met Thorpe's gaze.

"He did. I told her to be wary of him, but you know what Candy's like."

He didn't. His only memory was of a wide-eyed slip of a girl testifying in court. That was two years ago.

"Do you think she met up with him?"

"How the hell should I know? I don't think she would've done that, but..." She shrugged. "That girl has a mind of her own."

"We need to find Jesse Turner," Savage told Thorpe. He turned back to Martha. "Do you know where he lives?"

She shook her head, causing the smoke to swirl around her. "I only ever saw that loser when he came here with Candy."

"Never mind. We'll find him." Didn't Barbara say he had an ankle bracelet?

"You don't think he's harmed her, do you?" She couldn't stop her voice from wobbling. Maybe she did care about her daughter, after all. Savage caught a faint whiff of alcohol.

"I don't know." He didn't meet her gaze. "Thank you for your time, Martha. We'll be in touch." He turned to leave.

"You will find my Candy, won't you?" she called after him. "You'll bring her home?"

He studied the anxious woman. The last thing he wanted to do was make a promise he couldn't keep—and three days was a long time. "I'll do my best."

Thorpe headed for the Suburban, but Savage paused, drifting his gaze to a man across the road, watching them.

"What is it?" Thorpe asked.

"Hang five. I'll be right back."

Savage walked across the road to meet the man. He was much shorter than Savage, roughly five six or seven. He stood in front of a spacious mobile home painted a pale yellow with a white trim. Late forties, trimmed beard, hawkish nose, and sunglasses. His arms were crossed, his mouth curled into an amused grin.

"Zebadiah Swift," Savage said.

"Dalton Savage," the other man replied.

The two men shook hands. "I heard you'd taken over as sheriff. Congratulations."

"It's been a few years now." Last time they'd seen each other, Savage had just moved to Hawk's Landing and set his sights on the sheriff position.

"I kept meaning to drop by the station and say hi, but you know." He called it station, not sheriff's office, like the Denver cop he was.

"Yeah." Like Jasmine had said, life had gotten in the way. "So, how's business?"

"Good, mostly." Judging by the condition of the house, the smart SUV parked outside along with a shiny Harley-Davidson motorcycle, Savage could believe it. Zeb owned and lived in the trailer park. If anyone had a problem, they came to him.

Savage gave an approving nod. "I can see. How about your other business?"

Zeb looked affronted. "I don't know what you mean."

"Of course you don't." Savage hid a smirk. He'd heard of Zeb's lucrative little side hustle. Girls, operating out of three trailers behind the main house. Since they hadn't received any reports of bad behavior, Savage turned a blind eye. That might not always be the case. He shelved it for now. "You seen Candy Ray lately? Girl who lives across the street."

"No, but I heard she'd gone missing. Couple of days now." Zeb didn't look worried.

"Any idea where she might be?"

"Sorry, can't help you."

Why did Savage get the feeling his old friend wasn't telling him the whole truth? "If you know anything, Zeb, you should tell me. Her mother is worried about her."

Zeb's eyes shifted to the trailer across the road. "The only thing Martha's worried about is her stash of cigarettes, and what her new man gets up to when he's not with her."

"New man?" Savage followed Zeb's gaze.

"Yeah, guy's working at the farm out in Sun Valley. Spends his nights in Martha's bed, but when she works the late shift at the hotel, he likes to... How shall we say?"

"Wander across the road?" Savage finished for him.

"Yeah, that's right."

Savage thought for a moment. "Okay," he said. "Here's the deal. You tell me what you know about Candy, and I'll keep on pretending I don't know about your little side business."

Zeb's gaze darkened.

"Nothing goes on in this trailer park without your knowledge," Savage said. "So give." Thorpe watched them curiously from across the street. Savage liked his new deputy's intuitiveness.

Zeb sighed, his barrel chest heaving. For a small man, his shoulders were broader than expected. "You didn't hear it from me, but she's taken off into the mountains."

Savage frowned. "Which mountains?"

"Those ones." Zeb nodded towards the purple peaks in the distance. "She's gone hiking. Girl knows those peaks like the back of her hand. Grew up at the base of them. She's left town until things quiet down."

"What do you mean, quiet down?"

The man hesitated.

"Zeb?"

"Okay, okay." Zeb exhaled. "Candy came to see me the other night. She was freaking out about something. Said she had to get out, until things died down. I asked her what had happened, but she wouldn't tell me." At Savage's look, he added, "I swear, Dalton. I'm telling the truth."

"You mean she's not running because of Jesse Turner?"

"Jesse?" There was a pause. "He out of prison?"

"As of last week."

"Well, I'll be." Zeb scratched his chin. "That's an early parole, isn't it?"

"Yeah, overcrowding."

He shook his head. "I can believe it."

"You haven't seen him around here, have you?" Savage asked.

"No, not since that girl put him away a couple years back. What was it? Two or three years?"

Savage nodded. "Something like that."

"Took guts, that did." Zeb gave an approving nod. "We all knew the way he felt about her."

Savage looked him in the eye. "She did the right thing."

Zeb lowered his voice. "I heard she had no choice. That she was about to go down with him if she didn't testify. That true, Dalton?"

"I wouldn't know. Wasn't my case."

"No, that's right. It was your predecessor. He wasn't well liked around these parts."

Savage snorted. "Some things never change."

Zeb chuckled. "Now, if you don't mind, I'll be on my way."

"Why did she run?" Savage asked him.

Zeb gave him a warning look as if to say, "You don't wanna go there."

Savage refused to back down. "Why'd she take off into the mountains?"

"I told you, I don't know." Zeb didn't meet his gaze.

"Take a guess." Savage could tell Zeb was still holding back.

The ex-cop threw his hands up. "Something must have happened at the bar where she worked. That's all I can think of."

"The Roadhouse?"

"Yeah, that's it. She works behind the bar."

Mac's Roadhouse was a biker bar on the outskirts of town, on the road to Durango. Nobody knew who Mac was, but despite several changes in ownership, the name still appeared on the rusty tin sign outside.

"The Crimson Angels still use it as their HQ?" Savage asked.

"Hell yeah." He didn't need to say anything more. The Crimson Angels were, as their name suggested, a motorcycle club who had their leather-clad hands in a lot of different criminal pies. A bit like Zeb.

"You used to ride with them, didn't you?" Savage eyed the Harley-Davidson nestled under a tree beside the Chevy.

"Still do sometimes. I'm more of a recreational member."

"I didn't realize there were different levels of membership."

"Oh, yeah. It's like any other club."

"Not quite," Savage said. "Most clubs don't carry concealed weapons and settle disputes with their fists." The MC was a law unto itself. They refused to toe the line and were often involved in tiffs with law enforcement.

Zeb shrugged. He wasn't about to rat on anyone. It would be pointless pressing him.

"Okay," Savage relented, heading for the Suburban. "Thanks for the chat. If you hear anything else, give me a call. My cell's on the back of that card."

"About Candy?"

"About anything." Savage crossed the street again and jumped into the SUV.

"Who was that guy?" Thorpe asked.

"Someone I knew back in Denver. We worked together."

"A cop?" Thorpe glanced back at Zeb, who was walking into his house. "He doesn't look much like a cop."

Savage shrugged. "Used to be." They reversed out of the drive and headed toward the exit. "Until he got kicked out."

Thorpe's eyes grew large behind his glasses. "Seriously? What did he do?"

"Long story." He didn't elaborate and Thorpe knew better than to push.

Savage called Barbara as they drove out of the trailer park. The old man on the plastic chair stared at their SUV until it was off the property.

"Barbara, can you pull up the most recent address for Jesse Turner?"

"I don't have to pull it up." He heard her chair rolling across the floor. "I have it right in front of me."

"What, are you reading minds now?"

She snorted. "Actually, I was reading a cooking magazine about how to smoke a brisket, but then Parole called."

"Oh, yeah?" He frowned.

"Jesse Turner cut his bracelet."

"What?"

"He went offline three days ago, but as usual, they've only just let us know."

Typical.

"Three days," murmured Thorpe. Savage knew what he was thinking. The same day Candy Ray went missing.

"Last known address, then?"

"Sure, I'm sending it to your phone now." It beeped as the text came through.

"Thanks, Barbara."

He ended the call and turned to Thorpe. "Let's go find our suspect."

FOUR

JESSE TURNER LIVED in the middle of nowhere. The Suburban bumped along the rough, dirt track until they spotted a solitary house nestled behind some looming pines on the left. The spot was as deserted as they came. Savage could imagine tumbleweeds rolling across the dry land. It was so remote, they'd had to stop and ask for directions at a gas station. Luckily, the attendant knew Jesse.

"Not much around here." Thorpe stared out the window at the wilderness.

"Stretches all the way back to the foothills." Savage nodded toward the north mountains. "Plenty of hiking trails around here, and one or two ranches, but they're further that way."

Savage pulled into the driveway and cut the engine. They stepped out onto the gravel, the dust still settling.

"Looks more like a biker joint than a house," Thorpe said. He was right. The property was wide and squat, with a corrugated iron awning over the front porch. A double garage with roll-up doors adjoined the house, almost the same width, with a shed to the side. The Stars and Stripes flew above the awning. Out of sight, a dog snarled.

"Hope the dog's behind the fence." Thorpe glanced around.

They hadn't walked a step before a rough looking man around thirty-five flung the front door open, holding a shotgun.

"This is private property." He aimed the sawn-off at them. "I suggest you leave."

Savage held up his badge. "I'm Sheriff Savage from Hawk's Landing Sheriff's Department, and this is Deputy Thorpe. We want to talk to Jesse Turner. I believe this is his house?"

A pause as Savage's words sank in.

"Jesse ain't here."

"And you are?" Savage displayed the badge on his hip. His gun was inches away, and he itched to reach for it. It wasn't time yet.

"Blake Turner."

"Well, Blake, would you mind lowering the weapon? We just want to talk." He kept his hands out where the older Turner could see them. Beside him, Thorpe had turned into a statue.

Blake lowered the gun, just inches, but allowing them breathing space.

"Thank you. Do you know where Jesse went?" Savage asked.

Blake gave them a hard look. "I don't have to talk to you. Get off my property."

"We're law enforcement officers," Savage said. "We can come in and search your premises."

"Not without a warrant, you can't. I know my rights."

"This isn't your house," Savage said.

"This was my daddy's house," Blake replied. "I've got as much right to be here as anyone."

Unfortunately, he was right.

Savage turned to Thorpe. "Get on the phone. Call Parole. Jesse might still be inside."

Thorpe didn't move.

"Now," barked Savage. That seemed to wake him up. Thorpe hurried back to the SUV.

Savage shot Jesse's brother a hard look. "As soon as they get here, we're coming in."

Blake said nothing.

"You may as well save everybody some time and let us in. We just want to make sure Jesse isn't inside."

"He ain't here. I already told you that."

"If he's not here, then he's in violation of his parole. That's a serious offense. He could go back to prison."

Blake flinched.

"You can prevent that by telling us where he is," Savage said again.

"I'm tired of talking." Blake cocked the weapon. "I'm asking you one last time, get off my land before I make ya."

"You'd shoot at an unarmed law enforcement officer?" Savage shook his head. "Dumb move."

"You're carrying. I can see your sidearm." He nodded towards the holster at Savage's side.

"It's not in my hand," Savage said. *Not yet.*

What he wouldn't give to blow that shotgun right out of this idiot's hands.

"ETA twenty minutes," Thorpe called through the open window.

"Alright, you win." Savage backed away. "We'll wait for the parole officers to arrive. They don't need a warrant to search your house. Jesse is a fugitive from the law."

"You do that." Blake lowered the shotgun and disappeared back into the house.

"NICE GUY." Thorpe rolled his eyes. They walked back to the SUV.

"Just like his brother." Savage leaned back against the headrest. "Two years ago, Jesse Turner and two other guys held up a convenience store. An elderly man tried to intervene and got injured in the process. Luckily, he was alright, but Jesse had an assault charge added to the armed robbery rap. His girlfriend, Candy, testified against him."

Savage knew Thorpe would read the case file later, but right now, he needed the basics.

"Brave girl," Thorpe said.

"Yeah, but it might be why she was kidnapped."

"You really think Jesse's got her?"

"Timing's perfect," he said. "Jesse gets out four days ago, then cuts and runs on the same day as his ex-girlfriend goes missing. It's got to be related."

"Yeah, makes sense." Thorpe glanced at his notes. "Why'd he do it now, though? He's a free man. Well, almost. Why risk it all to go back to prison?"

"I can't answer that one." Savage shook his head. "Some people are just too dumb to know a good thing when they see it."

A roar of gravel made them both turn around. A patrol car raced up the drive. It pulled over with a screech of tires, and a robust man in khaki combat pants and a black T-shirt that said *Police Parole* on the back climbed out. He was armed with handcuffs, pepper spray, and a radio was attached to his belt.

"Dalton Savage?" He approached the Suburban.

Savage got out. "Yeah."

The men shook hands. "This is my deputy, James Thorpe."

Thorpe nodded from the other side of the vehicle.

"We need to search the premises," Savage explained. "And we haven't got time to get a warrant. We suspect Jesse Turner might be inside."

"He ain't here," the parole officer said. "We searched this place three days ago when he took off."

"We'd like to check that he hasn't come back." Savage was sure Jesse wasn't here, but it was good police work to make sure before they began searching all over the county.

"Suit yourself, that's all the reason I need."

He walked up to the front door, now locked. There was no sign of Blake or his shotgun.

The parole officer rapped on it several times. "Open up. We are going to search these premises."

Eventually, the door swung open. Savage and Thorpe had guns ready. No way they were letting the older Turner get the upper hand.

Blake stood there, glaring at them. Savage was pleased to see the shotgun standing to the side of the armchair, several yards away.

"If you could stand back, sir," the parole officer said. "We're conducting a search of the premises." The first thing he did was pick up Blake's weapon and disarm it. Then he turned to Blake. "Take a seat on the sofa, sir."

Blake scowled at them and sat down. He knew the drill. It was either that or be put in cuffs.

Savage and Thorpe followed him in. "You check the bedrooms and I'll do the rest of the house," he told his deputy. Thorpe gave a stiff nod and disappeared down the hallway.

Savage searched the kitchen, the garage, and the shed, but Jesse wasn't there. There were no signs of recent cohabitation either. No old cups of coffee, no clothing on the beds, or tools in the shed. The parolee had been gone a few days.

Three days was a long time.

"Told you he wasn't here," Blake smirked.

Savage turned to the man. "When did he leave?"

Blake looked defiant, but then he shrugged. "A couple of days ago."

"Do you know why?"

He stayed silent and looked away.

"Mr. Turner, if you know something and you don't tell us, we could haul you in for obstruction."

Blake scowled. "I don't know why he left, but he was pretty pissed when he did."

"He was angry?"

"Yeah, he got blind drunk, then the next day he got the wire cutters and snapped that thing off his ankle and took off." He shrugged. "I tried to stop him."

Not hard enough.

"Do you know where he went?" Savage asked.

"Nope. He didn't say nothing. Just jumped in his truck and high-tailed it out of here."

That didn't sound good.

It was looking more likely that Jesse Turner was their man. And if he was in that kind of mood when he left, there's no telling what he might have done to Candy.

FIVE

THE SUN HUNG low as Savage and Thorpe left Blake Turner's place to head towards town.

"I think you're right," Savage muttered, as the Suburban bounced along the gravel road. "Something set Jesse Turner off."

"It could've been his plan all along," Thorpe suggested. "To go after Candy, I mean."

Savage tapped his fingers on the steering wheel. "Could be, but like you said, why risk everything? In a year's time, he'd be a free man."

"Maybe he didn't want to wait a year?"

Savage grunted. "Maybe."

"I'm sending a list of Jesse's known associates," Barbara told them through the car speaker phone. "He might be hiding out with one of them."

"Thanks, Barbara."

Their phones buzzed at the same time as Barbara's message went through. Thorpe pulled up the list and read through it. "Larry 'Lick' Boone. I don't want to know how he got that nickname."

"It's on account of him taking a licking and keeping on ticking," Savage supplied. "He's a big fella, two-hundred and fifty pounds of muscle gone to fat, but resilient. He can take one hell of a beating. I've seen three men battle to put him down."

"You know him?" Thorpe glanced across.

Savage grunted. "We've had a few run-ins. He's a petty criminal, low level. It's his fists you've got to watch out for."

"Thanks for the tip. So, we're going to question him about Jesse?"

"That's the plan."

Thorpe nodded and went back to the list. It wasn't long. Jesse had been away too long to have many contacts in Hawk's Landing. "Most of these guys have moved on," Thorpe said, eyeing the addresses.

"Let's start with Lick and see where that leads us." Savage pulled off the gravel road onto the asphalt. The smooth road was a welcome relief.

They followed the satnav to a suburb on the far side of town. Thorpe stared out of the window as they slowed down to avoid a scraggly looking dog that ran across the road. "I've never been to this part of town," Thorpe said.

"You're not missing much."

Rundown houses, weathered porches, and overgrown yards. A broken white picket fence dream. The economic downturn had hit this community hard. "Most of these folk are earning minimum wage," Savage said. "Working two or three jobs just to survive."

They passed a low-cost apartment block with a group of teenagers lurking outside. "We've had some trouble there before," Savage murmured. "Mostly drug-related violence."

"Boone's house should be around the next corner." Thorpe checked the map on the navigation system.

They turned right and spotted two men huddled outside a dirty white clapboard house. One had a wrestler's build, the other slender and weedy, his arms covered in tattoos. It was obvious from their secretive stance that something shady was going on.

"That's him." Savage nodded to the men, keeping his hands on the wheel. "The big guy with the baseball cap."

The men glanced up at the approaching Suburban, then the slender one yelled, "It's five-O!" They split up, sprinting in different directions.

Without a word, Savage leaped from the car and took off in pursuit of Boone. He knew Thorpe would give chase in the Suburban. An excellent driver, Thorpe could handle almost anything on wheels. Savage had seen Thorpe take the SUV off-road at high speeds in a raging storm, and smash through fences to get where he needed to go.

Lick Boone used all his height and strength to pummel himself across the asphalt. He was fast too, faster than his bulky frame suggested. Savage sped after him, soon panting as his chest burned. He'd always thought he was in good shape for a guy in his forties. Now he wasn't so sure.

Boone rounded a corner and weaved through the parked cars like a boxer until he exited back to the sidewalk. The houses were more spread out here, bigger, but just as badly maintained. Savage put on a burst of speed, willing his legs to move faster. Lactic acid started to build, and he clenched his teeth against the pain. He'd almost caught up to the thug when Boone vaulted over a low wooden fence and scampered across a garden.

Damn.

Savage followed but caught his shoe on the top slat and went sprawling across the lawn. Growling, he got up and kept going, hurdling a low dividing wall into the neighbor's yard. A cocker spaniel gave a surprised yelp as Savage raced past.

Savage forced his way through a dried-up thorn bush into a third garden, only to spot Boone entering the house through an open sliding door.

Hell no.

Savage followed, darting through someone's living room. The toddler watching TV didn't even glance up. He raced through the kitchen and out the back, into a weed-ridden yard.

"Boone, stop!" he yelled, but the big guy barged straight through a knee-high wooden gate that flew off its hinges into the road. Savage was losing ground.

He debated pulling his weapon and shooting the bastard in the leg to slow him down, but there was no just cause. As far as he could tell, Boone wasn't carrying.

Then he heard a crunch of tires and looked up. The Suburban came hurtling down the street. Thorpe flew past him, kicking up gravel as he floored the eight-cylinder engine. Savage watched as the SUV chased down the fleeing man until he was pinned in a dead end.

Thank you, Thorpe.

Dipping into his last energy reserves, Savage took off down the street after them, gun drawn.

"Put your hands where I can see them!" he shouted. The big guy had barely worked up a sweat.

Boone glared at him like a caged animal, then his giant shoulders sank. There was nowhere else to run. In front of them stood a warehouse surrounded by a high barbed wire fence. Trapped.

The fugitive complied, sticking his hands in the air.

Savage stormed up. "Why the hell did you run? We only want to talk to you."

The man shifted, not making eye contact.

Thorpe jumped out of the car, sidearm ready. He approached slowly, keeping his gun steady. That's when Savage got it. The guy was dealing or buying. That's what the huddle was all about.

He nodded to Thorpe who holstered his weapon and conducted a search. In the right front pocket, he found a small bag of white powder. It looked like coke.

"Thought as much," Thorpe murmured.

"It's not mine." Boone gesticulated wildly. "That guy made me take it when you arrived."

"Well, it's on your person." Savage shrugged. "According to the law, that makes it yours." Boone let off a rant of expletives colorful enough to turn Thorpe's cheeks pink.

Savage ignored him and took out his cuffs. "I'm afraid you're coming with us."

"No man, I ain't done anything." He fought against the cuffs, but Thorpe drew his sidearm and held it against the man's head.

"Easy, now," Thorpe said.

Boone glowered at him but stopped wriggling long enough for Savage to get the cuffs on.

"Hey, man. That's too tight."

Savage didn't respond. Instead, he called for a cage car. If this guy kicked off, he'd be too much for one of them to manage if the other was driving.

A short while later, Littleton arrived to transport Boone, still yelling obscenities at them.

"He's all yours." Savage handed the big man over. The lanky deputy, flushed with excitement, locked Boone in the back. "Shall I book him?"

The big guy thumped on the cage door. "This ain't fair. I didn't do nothing."

"Yeah, process him and let him simmer down overnight. We can interview him in the morning."

"You're not coming back with us, Sheriff?" Littleton asked.

Savage shook his head. "There's something I've got to do."

Don't forget the scan at five.

SIX

SAVAGE ROARED into the parking lot at the doctor's office and pulled into the first spot he could find. It was ten past five—slightly late. Leaping from the SUV, he ran toward the building, just missing a young mother with a toddler in tow.

"Sorry!" he called, side-skipping them.

He burst in, startling the receptionist, and earning himself an exasperated look from Becca, still in the waiting room.

"Sorry I'm late." He slumped against the counter to catch his breath. His heart was still pounding from the mad dash through the streets.

Becca took in his flushed face, the dirt stains on his knees, and the grazes on his hands. "What on earth happened to you?"

He dusted himself off. "Nothing, just a little fall. I'm good."

She frowned and was about to reply when the receptionist's desk phone beeped. "You can go through now." She peered at them over her computer.

"Looks like you had an interesting day." Becca got to her feet. Unlike him, she looked amazing in a smart skirt and white, silk blouse, her hair swept back in a silver clip. Dark tendrils had escaped and caressed her face. He was almost afraid to touch her in case he sullied her.

Becca had just gotten in from working a half day at the Somers Institute, an inpatient facility for challenged youth in Pagosa Springs, an hour's drive from Hawk's Landing. She was a founder and lead psychiatrist.

"You could say that."

Candy Ray. Blake Turner. Lick Boone.

A wave of weariness washed over him, and he swayed.

She frowned. "You sure you're okay?"

He was hobbling from pulling a muscle during his chase after Boone, but Becca was trained to notice these things. As a psychiatrist, she was an expert on body language, and subtle nuances that people didn't even know they portrayed.

"Yeah, just a bit stiff." Savage grimaced and stretched his arms out, clicking his back.

Becca crossed her arms over her chest. "Dalton, what happened?"

"I'm fine."

One look, that's all it took for him to give in. It was useless to keep anything from her.

"Fine. I chased a guy a couple of blocks across town. I'm feeling it, that's all. Not as young as I used to be."

She studied him, her head tilted to one side. "Did you catch him?"

"Actually, no. Thorpe pinned him down in the Suburban. The guy's in custody."

She frowned. "Does this have anything to do with that missing person?"

"Indirectly. He's an associate of the guy we think kidnapped her." While he couldn't go into detail, he trusted Becca enough to discuss aspects of the case with her.

They paused outside the assessment room where the obstetrician waited to do the scan. Becca looked at him. "Her? It's a young woman?"

"Yeah, twenty-two years old."

She cringed. "Does the man you were chasing know where she is?"

"Maybe. We haven't questioned him yet."

Becca gave a short nod. "This won't take long."

To hell with getting her dirty. He hugged her hard, then rested his hands on her shoulders. "That man isn't going anywhere. Besides, it'll do him good to cool off in the cell overnight. Tomorrow will be soon enough."

"Becca?" The doctor opened the door. "Please, come in. It's good to see you both." Her gaze fell to Becca's bump. "How have you been?"

Savage let her go. Becca turned to the doctor, a smile on her lips. "I'm good, thank you."

"Any problems?"

"Not that I know of."

"Great." She laid out her utensils on the pull-out shelf nearby. "Slip on the robe and climb onto the bed. I'll be back in a minute." Pulling the curtain around the cubicle, she went back to her desk to give Becca some privacy.

"A missing girl is also important." Becca disappeared behind the screen to change.

Savage waited outside the curtain. The obstetrician cast a furtive glance in his direction. He could only imagine what she must be thinking. How could a fine, well-dressed woman like Becca have this uncouth, dirty man for a partner?

He smiled at her and tried to release some of the tension in his neck. It wasn't just the investigation that had him so uptight. His stomach was doing flip-flops at the thought of seeing his unborn baby.

This wasn't the first scan he'd witnessed. The scan at twelve-weeks had been mind-blowing, seeing the tiny, perfectly formed human being in Becca's stomach. This time, he knew what to expect. Even so, his heart beat a little faster as Becca climbed onto the gurney and the doctor began the procedure.

"You're worried about her, aren't you?" Becca said, as a dark, wobbly image appeared on the screen. The nurse shifted the probe on Becca's belly for a clearer picture. Some of the fuzziness disappeared and the shape of the fetus came into view. He could make out the curvature of the spine, the tiny arms and legs.

He nodded. "The suspect's a parolee who got early release. He sent her threatening letters from prison. She's the one who put him away."

"She turned him in?"

"Testified against him."

Becca breathed in. "That's a motive, for sure."

"Yeah." His eyes were glued to the screen. The baby looked like it was sucking its thumb. "She was last seen three days ago."

"Three days?" Becca pursed her lips. She knew as well as he did that with every passing day, the chances of finding the victim alive decreased exponentially. Every second counted.

"Everything looks normal," the obstetrician interrupted, perturbed that they weren't showing as much interest in the scan as they were in each other. "You have a healthy baby there."

Savage reached for Becca's hand as they registered the doctor's words. A surge of emotion hit him in the chest. Joy. Relief. He gave her hand a squeeze. "That's wonderful news."

Becca stared at the curled-up black and white image, the tiny heart pulsing in the middle. "It's still so surreal."

He knew what she meant. It was like they were watching a movie, something that couldn't possibly be a reality for them.

"Is it a girl or a boy?" Becca whispered.

Savage hadn't given much thought to the sex of the baby. Being a father was more than enough to get his head around, but Becca didn't like surprises. She preferred to be prepared.

"I can't see from this angle. Bear with me." She manipulated the probe.

"You sure you don't need to go back in tonight?" Becca's attention was back on Savage.

"No, it'll take a while to process him. Even if he gave us something tonight, there's nothing we could do until the morning. I'll go in early tomorrow." He just hoped it wouldn't be too late.

"You'll find her," Becca said.

"I know. I just can't help thinking—"

"Don't." She pressed down on his hand. "Don't do that. You're doing everything you can."

"I hope so." He forced himself to relax. She was right, as usual. There was no point in worrying about what could happen. If Candy was alive, he'd find her. It was just a matter of time.

The obstetrician cleared her throat. They both turned to look at her.

"It's a boy."

SEVEN

"IS HE READY?" Savage asked Barbara, as he walked into the lobby early the next morning. The sun was barely up, but he'd called the admin assistant last night and told her to come in early with him to prepare Boone for interrogation.

"He's been fed and watered." She rolled her eyes. "Got a mouth on him, that one." Regulations meant they had to make sure their suspects' basic needs were taken care of. They wouldn't let the guy starve, even though losing some weight might not be the worst thing for him.

"Tell me about it. Should have heard him when he was arrested." Savage scanned in and pushed open the door. "Thanks Barbara."

Deputy Littleton was already typing at his desk, typing slowly and methodically, an expression of the utmost concentration on his face. He'd been here a year now and still hadn't gotten any faster.

A boy. Savage was still taking it in. Now, the unborn fetus had a gender. An identity. They'd spent a fun few hours last night brainstorming names, but hadn't come up with anything they both loved.

Littleton glanced up. "You sure you need me to sit in, Sheriff?"

Savage forced his attention back. "Yeah. One day you'll do these yourself."

Littleton swallowed. Interrogating suspects wasn't one of his strong points. Savage was still trying to figure out exactly what was, but in the meantime, the rookie needed as much experience as he could get. Besides, Savage would be lying if he said he didn't have an ulterior motive. Boone was a bully, that much was obvious. He'd take pleasure in putting Littleton down, which Savage could take advantage of.

"Okay," Littleton squeaked.

"I'll go get him. Wait here."

Littleton was only too happy to oblige.

Savage went through a door at the back, then down the narrow hall, past the stairs to the basement where they kept all the files, and into the booking room.

He passed through the secure door to the other side, to the cells, making sure to shut the door behind him. The clang echoed down the hallway. He heard Lick before seeing him.

"Hey man, is that you? I've been here all night. You gonna charge me, or what?"

"Morning," Savage drawled, coming to a stop in front of the cell. Lick stood in front of the aluminum bed bolted to the concrete wall. "Sleep well?"

Lick replied in expletives.

"We're going to have ourselves a little chat." Savage held up the handcuffs. "Come over and turn around."

Lick did as he was told, swearing under his breath. After snapping the cuffs on, Savage instructed the man to stand back as he opened the cell.

Holding the big man firmly by the arm, he led him back down the hallway, through the booking room, and into the narrow corridor where the two interview rooms were located. The two doors were marked Interview 1 and Interview 2, although they seldom needed both.

Savage opened the door to Interview 1 and led Lick inside. "Wait here."

"Don't rush. I got all day," Lick called after him, his voice heavy with sarcasm.

Savage locked him in, then went back to his office to get the case file. There wasn't much in it, but it always unnerved the suspect to think the sheriff's office had detailed notes on them. On the way back, he stopped by Littleton's desk.

"You ready?"

The thin deputy gave a nervous nod.

Savage studied his pale face. "He's going to go for you," he warned, "but follow my lead, okay?"

Littleton gulped, his expression confused. He had no idea what was coming. "Okay."

They went in.

Boone sulked at the metal table. His handcuffs clicked against the surface as he shifted to glare at them.

Savage ignored him and sat down. Littleton did the same, shooting a timid glance at the beefy drug thug.

Savage rustled through the case folder and studied Boone's criminal record. Littleton had pulled it from the state database. The heavy man peered across the table, trying to read it upside down.

Savage nodded at Littleton who looked like he was about to pass out. Boone gave a smirk. Savage carried on reading, not bothering to acknowledge the suspect who leaned back in his chair, waiting for the first question.

Littleton cleared his throat, but his voice hadn't lost its squeak. "When did you last see Jesse Turner?"

Boone rubbed his temples, confused. "Huh?"

"I said, when did you last—"

"I heard what you said," Boone snarled. "Why you askin' me about him?"

Savage looked up, surprised. "Oh, you thought this was about you?" He glanced at Littleton and back to the suspect. "No, we're looking for your pal, Jesse Turner. He broke his parole."

Boone looked away, boot faced. "I don't know where Jesse is. I haven't seen him since he went inside some two years ago."

"I see." Savage turned to Littleton. "You see how he looked away? He won't look me in the eye."

Littleton nodded.

"That means he's lying."

"I ain't lying," Boone bellowed, thumping his fists on the table, the cuffs jarring.

"But you do know Jesse Turner?"

"Yeah, I know him, but I got no idea where he is. I didn't even know he was out."

"See how he answered that?" Savage interrupted. "Now, did that sound like he was telling the truth?"

"Uh, no?" Littleton responded, unsure.

"Exactly." Savage pursed his lips and shifted his gaze back to Boone. "And did you notice that little twitch at the corner of his eye? He's still lying to us."

Boone sat sullenly, glaring at them.

Savage's phone buzzed. He reached for it and read the message, letting the silence draw out. Littleton was sweating now, while Boone resembled a petulant child who'd been caught with his hand in the cookie jar.

"Now that is interesting," Savage muttered, as if speaking to himself.

"What is?" Boone leaned forward.

"It says here that Jesse's ankle bracelet put him at your house a day and a half ago." Savage met Boone's gaze across the table. "That's what we call evidence, so we can prove you were lying to us."

Boone glanced down at his hands, now in his lap.

"What was Jesse Turner doing at your house, Lick?"

No answer.

Savage sighed. "You're looking at a cocaine distribution charge. You ready to go back inside?"

"I wasn't dealing," Boone said. "That was for personal use."

"I'm not sure a judge will see it that way."

Boone shook his head. "You can't pin a distribution rap on me when I wasn't dealing."

Savage prodded the file in front of him with his finger. "With your history, no one will believe you. Your best bet is to help us with Jesse Turner."

"And then what?" Boone sulked.

"And then we'll see what we can do about your drug charge."

There was a stilted pause as Lick thought this over. Would he rat out his friend in exchange for his own freedom? Savage was betting he would. "Okay, man. Jesse came to my place madder than a hornet."

"Why's that?"

"Why's what?"

"Why was he mad?"

"Er..." Boone looked away.

"Do you need me to repeat the question?"

"He was looking for someone."

Savage met Littleton's gaze.

"Who was he looking for?" Littleton asked.

The gaze shifted. "Candy, his ex."

Savage nodded. "Why was he looking for her?"

"I don't know. He didn't tell me much."

"What *did* he tell you?"

Boone sighed and tried to rock back on the metal chair, but it was bolted to the ground. "He saw a picture of her on Instagram with another dude."

"Another dude?" This was the first he'd heard. "I thought she was Jesse's ex."

Lick shrugged. "That don't mean he don't still have feelings for her."

"Feelings? He was sending her hate mail from prison."

"Hey, you asked me what I know. That's what he said. He was mad as hell. Stormed off like he was ready to kill someone."

Interesting choice of words.

"Would he harm her?" Savage asked.

Lick's forehead creased, and he waved his hands in the air, as much as he could with the cuffs on. "No way. Jesse was crazy about Candy. He'd never hurt her."

"The restraining order she laid against him three years ago says different," Savage pointed out.

Lick shut up.

"Did he say where he was going? Did he know where she was?"

"He said he was heading up to the ridge. Apparently, that's where the pictures were taken."

"Stony Ridge?"

"Yeah."

"That's quite a hike." Not many people made it up there. Most only went part of the way on account of the height, rough terrain, and time it took to get all the way to the point. It was a full day's hike at a steady pace. Not something that could be done in one afternoon.

Boone shrugged. "Wouldn't know."

"Okay, so let's get this straight. Jesse Turner came to your place. Why? What did he want from you?"

Lick dropped his gaze to the table.

"He did it again," Littleton pointed out. "He looked away."

"He sure did." Savage allowed himself a tiny smirk.

"Okay, jeez. He wanted to borrow my brother's hiking gear. He used to be in the military, so we got all that stuff lying around at home."

Savage spread his hands. "Was that so hard? Why couldn't you just tell us that in the first place?"

Lick hesitated, then sighed. "I didn't tell you because that wasn't the only thing he borrowed from me."

Savage looked at him. "What else did he take?"

Boone looked back down at his hands. "He took my gun."

EIGHT

"THE GUY'S ARMED," Savage told the rest of the team once he'd finished the interview and released Lick with a warning.

"He's hunting her." Sinclair's brow creased with worry. Becky Sinclair was in her late twenties, and one of the hardest working deputies Savage had ever met. She'd more than proven herself over the last couple of years. If he wanted something done right, he gave it to Sinclair.

"Jesse's brother said he'd seen a photo of Candy with another guy on Instagram. Took a while, but I found it."

Savage gave her an incredulous look. "How?"

She grinned. "I looked for hashtags relating to the Stony Ridge trail going back three days, and bingo."

Savage peered over her shoulder.

"It is Candy, isn't it?" she asked.

Thorpe popped his head up from behind his computer and studied the image of the young woman with wild blond hair, tanned skin, and laughing blue eyes. "That's her alright. Who's she with?"

It was a selfie shot, slightly awkward, but they were both smiling. Candy had her arm draped around a dark-haired man's shoulders. He had glasses, angular facial features, and about a day's worth of stubble. The accompanying caption read, "Meeting cool people on the trail."

"Mark Stillwater, I think." Sinclair scrolled up to the top. "It's posted on his page, anyway."

"That must be the guy Jesse saw." Savage perched on the desk and studied the photograph. "Name doesn't sound familiar." Hawk's Landing was a small town.

"According to this, he works for Blue Mountain Travel, a tourist company in Colorado Springs. Their website has a large hiking section and rates all the trails. He must be down here for work."

Savage inspected each detail of the photograph. Shorts, plain T-shirt, high quality backpack. The guy was a seasoned hiker.

"What's that?" Savage asked, pointing to a shiny, gold label on the side of the pack.

Sinclair zoomed in. "It looks like a metallic keyring. I think it says Colorado Springs."

"That makes sense," Thorpe said.

"Have we contacted the company?" Savage asked. "They might be able to give us his number."

"You mean he might still be with Candy?" Sinclair asked.

Savage shrugged. "Who knows, but it's worth a shot."

They waited while Sinclair called the travel company. She was put through to a man identifying as Mark's boss.

"This is Deputy Sinclair from Hawk's Landing Sheriff's Department," she said. "I'm trying to contact one of your employees, Mark Stillwater. Could you give me his contact information?"

She listened, then took down a number. "Thank you." She hung up the phone and looked at Savage. "Got it."

Savage picked up his phone and dialed. Straight to voicemail.

"Damn." He shook his head.

"Phone's switched off or out of range," Thorpe said. "Maybe try him again later. Reception comes and goes in the mountains."

"What about Candy?" Sinclair asked.

"We know she's heading up to the ridge," Savage said.

"Still, there are lots of ways to get there."

Savage raised an eyebrow.

Sinclair shrugged. "What? I used to hike a lot with my dad."

Savage didn't know that about her.

"Maybe we can narrow it down. Thorpe, have you managed to find her phone?"

The deputy picked up a remote control and pressed a couple of buttons. A mounted flat screen on the wall lit up and showed a topographical map.

"This is a map of the mountains, including the hiking trails," Thorpe said, pulling up the cellphone data and superimposing it onto the map. This was Thorpe's strong point. He loved making sense from data. "And this is Candy's geolocation up until yesterday, when her phone lost signal."

Savage ground his jaw. He didn't want to think about what that meant.

"The data puts her around Beaver Brook when her phone lost service." Thorpe pointed the cursor on a squiggly blue line. "It funnels through Glacier Gorge further down the mountain and ends up as a lake at the bottom."

An inset photograph showed a pristine blue lake, semi-iced over and glittering in the bright sunlight. The photo was from the winter. It was late spring now, and the lake would be dark and deep.

"What's that darker area next to the brook?" Littleton asked.

"Forest," Thorpe said, adjusting his glasses. "Hundreds of acres of it. It won't be easy finding her in that."

"What about Jesse's phone?" Savage was thinking out loud. "Were we able to trace that?"

"Yeah, briefly, before we lost the signal completely." Thorpe pressed a button on the remote control and changed the image. Candy's cellphone data disappeared, replaced by a red glowing dot. He shrugged. "This is Jesse Turner's last known location."

"That's close to where Candy was, isn't it?" Sinclair asked. "Look, that's the same brook, right?"

Savage was thinking the same thing.

"Yeah." Thorpe brought Candy's location back up, so both were visible on the map. "They're close, but not intersecting."

Not yet.

"Still, it's something to go on." Savage stood. "If this was yesterday, he may have found her by now."

"What are we going to do?" Littleton asked.

"We're going up to get her." Savage headed back to his desk. "Saddle up, team. We're going hiking."

"Don't we need equipment?" Littleton's voice squeaked, the way it did when he was nervous.

"We're not camping overnight," Savage said. "But you have time to go home and pick up the basics. Backpack, water, a snack, maybe."

Littleton swayed a little.

"There's a hiking store on the way out of town," Sinclair told him as they left the office. She put an arm on Littleton's shoulder. "I'll come with you."

He shot her a grateful smile.

Savage strode past Barbara's desk. "Stand by, Barbara. We'll let you know if we find anything."

"Will do." She beamed at him. "I hope you find that girl and bring her home safe."

So do I.

They parked in the lot at the base of the mountain. From there, the trailhead wound up the foothills, getting steeper until it reached a plateau. According to the map, there were multiple trails leading off in different directions. Some were looped trails that followed scenic routes past creeks and waterfalls. Others, aimed at the more seasoned hiker, ascended through rougher terrain. Most had forested sections as the woodlands covered a vast majority of this side of the mountain.

"Everybody ready?" Savage called, as they wriggled into their backpacks and pulled on their caps.

They were about to set off when Savage's phone buzzed. "Savage."

He listened carefully, while the others waited. "Okay, thanks for letting me know. We're about to head up, so we'll meet you there."

He hung up.

"What happened?" Sinclair could read him better than the others.

"That was State Patrol," he said, his face grim. "They found a body in the mountains."

Sinclair gasped. "Is it her?"

"No, it's a male."

"You think it's related?" Thorpe asked.

"I have no idea, but it's close enough to be a concern. Come on, let's head out. I told them we'd meet them there."

"What about Candy?" Sinclair asked. "We can't abandon her."

"We're not." He set off, taking long strides towards the trailhead. "But the homicide could be related. We need to at least rule it out."

She nodded and said, "Okay." But he could tell she wasn't happy.

"We'll find Candy," he said over his shoulder.

He only hoped they weren't too late.

NINE

THEY SPOTTED the crime scene long before they reached it. Even through the shadows cast by the dense foliage, they spotted white-clad forensic experts traipsing around, collecting evidence and photographing the area.

Savage called a halt and gave his team a rest. They doubled over, catching their breath. He was also panting, but he'd set a grueling pace to get there with time to spare. They needed to search for Candy while it was still light. After taking a long drink from his water canister, he strode up to an officer.

"Sheriff Savage, Hawk's Landing Sheriff's Department. One of your guys called me a couple hours ago." It had taken them most of the morning to get here.

"Yeah, that was me. Captain Birch, good to meet you." They shook hands.

"What have you got?" Savage asked.

"He's over here." Birch stepped off the path and fought his way through the thick brush. It sloped downwards, towards the creek that could just be heard in the background. Savage followed, stepping carefully on the plastic steps that prevented contamination. He began to understand why it had taken them so long to process the scene.

"A hiker found him when his pooch sniffed out the body," Birch said. "Otherwise, he'd have been there for weeks, even months. It's so thick we had to cut a path to get to him."

The victim lay on his stomach, arms above his head as if he'd been dragged from the path. Savage bent down to get a closer look. Dirty hiking shorts, torn T-shirt, limbs covered in scratches. It was hard to know whether they resulted from the attack or a previous misadventure. Savage assumed the former.

The man's face was partially hidden, but the visible areas were covered in mud and moss stains. There was a bloody wound on the back of his head.

"Blunt force trauma?" Savage asked.

Birch gave a sober nod. "Yeah, looks like repeated blows. It was a vicious attack. The ME is on his way, but it'll take him a while. The ATV can only get as far as the rest point." While the all-terrain vehicle was useful for the lower reaches, it couldn't traverse rocky tracks or forested areas where branches and tree stumps crossed the path.

Savage remembered the exquisite viewing point they'd passed on the trek here. Had the victim paused to stare out over it before he was bludgeoned to death? He peered into the foliage. "No murder weapon?"

"Nope, not yet. Once the ME gets here, we'll have a better idea of what was used to kill him."

Savage bent down to take a closer look at the wound. The surface area was large and jagged, from a heavy object like a rock or the butt of a revolver. Birch was right, it wasn't just one blow that had done this. There was anger behind this attack, and plenty of it.

Lick had told them exactly what gun Jesse had stolen from his house. It could be used as a striking object, but would it have caused this much damage?

"Hopefully, the CSI team will find it." Jesse could have hidden it amongst the thick vegetation. "I take it you're going to process the entire area?"

"Yeah, once they get there. We'd look for it, but we don't want to compromise the body. We'll tear the scene apart after the ME takes the body away."

Savage gave a curt nod. It was the right course of action. "Keep me posted."

"What's your interest in the John Doe?" Birch asked.

"Could be related to a missing person's case we're working on," Savage said. "We've also got a parolee on the run, but this isn't him."

"We're getting an ID now," said one of the patrol officers holding a battery-operated device. Savage recognized it as a portable AFIS machine, a fingerprinting device that could be transported to crime scenes for quick identification, provided the victim was in the system. "Bingo."

Savage arched an eyebrow.

"The victim is Mark Stillwell. From Colorado Springs."

"Mark Stillwell?" That name sounded familiar. "Mark Stillwell! I know him, or I've seen him before on Instagram. He was with our missing person."

"It's not looking good for your missing person, if *he's* turned up dead." Birch nodded at the victim.

No, this didn't bode well. Savage didn't need the Police Captain to tell him that.

"Got an address?" Birch asked the officer.

"Yes, sir."

"Send someone over to talk to his relatives. Let's find out what he was doing on the trail."

"Could be work-related." Savage raked a hand through his salt and pepper hair. "He worked at a travel company that specializes in ranking hiking trails."

"And you know this, how?"

"His social media profile. I can get my deputy to send you the details, if you like."

Birch grunted. "That would be good, thanks."

The medical examiner arrived, and the officers gave him space to work. He inspected the body, took samples from around the head wound and under the fingernails, and then bagged the hands and feet. He'd send the shoes to the lab for analysis and take more samples from the man's fingernails to check for DNA.

Savage conferred with his team. "It's not looking good. Stillwell's dead, Candy's still missing."

"Are we assuming the two are related?" Thorpe asked.

"Could be." He scratched his chin. "If Jesse Turner found them..."

"You think he could have beaten the victim to death?" Sinclair asked. "He's a small-time crook and drug dealer. Not a murderer."

"He was pretty mad when he left," Thorpe pointed out.

"And he had a beef against Candy," Savage added.

"Do you think he's got her now?" Sinclair bit her lip.

"It's likely." He turned back to the ME. "What was the time of death?"

"I'd say no more than twenty-four hours ago."

Savage frowned. "Yesterday. This was after the picture was taken, but Jesse could have caught up with them. We have to keep looking."

Thorpe glanced up at the sky, or what he could see of it between the trees. "It'll be dark soon." Already, the shadows were lengthening and the temperature dropping.

They watched as the ME and his assistant loaded the victim's body onto a gurney. Savage stared at the pale, waxy face. Poor guy. His only mistake on the trail was meeting Candy.

Sinclair shivered and wrapped her arms around herself.

A thought struck Savage.

"No backpack," he said out loud. The others glanced at him. "In the picture, he was wearing a backpack. Don't you remember?"

"Hang on." Thorpe pulled up his phone. He'd taken a screenshot of the photograph of Candy in it. They all studied it. Mark Stillwell had been wearing a khaki backpack.

"What about his glasses?" said Thorpe. "They weren't on the body either."

"Could have fallen off when he was murdered," Savage said. "I'll find out." He walked back to where the captain was standing. The CSI team had begun processing the scene. Half a dozen white-clad technicians were on their hands and knees, scrutinizing every blade of grass. He couldn't claim they weren't being thorough.

"This is the guy." Savage showed Birch the photograph. "You're looking for a khaki backpack, pair of glasses, and a mobile phone. He used it to post the pictures before he was killed."

"Gotcha," Birch said. "I'll let the team know."

"Could you keep us in the loop? We'd really like to take a look at his phone if you find it."

"Will do."

They shook hands.

"We'd better get going," Savage told the others. "We only have a couple hours of daylight left."

He got a nod from Sinclair and Thorpe, although Littleton stifled a moan. He was very much out of his comfort zone. "You okay, Littleton?"

"Oh, sorry. Yes, boss." He glanced around him as if he expected something to jump out of the bushes at any moment.

"Good, let's get moving then. We don't have much time."

They followed the trail out of the forest and to the location Candy's phone had pinged before the signal was lost. The earth turned crumbly beneath their feet and the incline steepened. They slipped and slid and grasped onto boulders and submerged roots to keep their footing. The deepening darkness didn't help.

All four of them turned on their flashlights to illuminate the way. In addition, Savage wore an LED headlamp. Littleton, at the back, gave a yelp and slid several yards down the mountain. Reluctantly, Savage called a halt.

They weren't making any headway. There was nothing up ahead to indicate that Candy had passed through here. No campfire, no items of clothing, no blood on the trail. Nothing but the hard ground and the descending chill.

"Okay, let's call it a day," Savage said, as they huddled together. "It's dangerous to go any further."

"What about Candy?" Sinclair whispered. "She's out here somewhere."

"We're no good to her if we go tumbling down the mountain," Savage pointed out.

Still brushing himself off, Littleton grunted in agreement.

"Let's come back tomorrow. We'll start at daybreak."

Sinclair glanced at Thorpe, who nodded.

Savage turned around. His light picked up a flash of glass lying to the side of the trail. Sinclair saw it, too. "What's that?" she asked.

Savage walked over to inspect the object. "It's a phone."

They crowded around, studying the cracked screen partially hidden under scattered leaves. "Candy's," Sinclair said.

Savage took a glove out of his pack and picked up the phone. Thorpe marked their location with a little flag, forcing it into the hard ground. It had a transponder on it in case they couldn't find their way back to it tomorrow.

"I'll run the phone when we get back to the station," Thorpe said. "It might tell us something."

"Let's head back. We can't go any further tonight." Savage peeled the glove off, enveloping the cell phone, then placed it in his backpack.

Turning around, they headed down the way they'd come.

TEN

IT WAS NEARLY midnight when Savage let himself into the house.

They'd gone back to the station and taken a look at Candy's cellphone, but Thorpe hadn't been able to open it. The five-digit pass code made it impossible.

"We'll need a hacker," Thorpe had said. "I'll have to ask the state police IT department what they can do." That's where they'd left it.

A floorboard creaked and Savage paused, cringing.

"Dalton, is that you?" Becca's voice echoed down the hallway from the bedroom.

"Sorry. I was trying not to wake you."

"I'm awake anyway."

He walked into the bedroom to find her sitting up in bed, illuminated by the soft glow of the bedside lamp. An open book lay on the cover beside her.

"It's good to see you." He sank down next to her with a groan.

"How'd it go?" She rubbed his back. God, that felt good. He was bone tired from the hike, on top of the stiffness he still carried from yesterday's chase.

"We didn't find her." He faced his fiancé. "We think her ex has got her up in the mountains."

"Is that where you've been?" She raised an eye at the thin layer of trail dust on his clothing.

"Yeah. State police found a body on the trail to Stony Ridge. We think it's related."

Becca sat up straight, a frown on her face. "Related? How?"

He sighed. "It's a long story, but the girl posted a picture of herself and the dead guy on social media, which provoked her ex into going after her."

"Is he still in love with her?" Becca asked.

"Obsessed, more like. He's been inside for over two years."

Becca blinked at him. "You think he killed this hiker in some crazy revenge attack?"

Savage kicked off his boots. Dust covered every inch of his body, even his eyes felt grainy. "It looks that way."

"And now he's got her."

"Yeah." He dropped his head against Becca's shoulder as a surge of weariness hit him.

Becca wrapped her arms around him in a warm hug. He closed his eyes, savoring the moment. She smelled so good, unlike him, and he resisted the urge to take her in his arms. "You tried your best."

"Yeah, but it's not good enough. We need to find her before it's... before it's too late."

"You think he'll hurt her?"

Savage shrugged. "He's got a gun, and the guy we found—" He looked away.

"What?"

"His head had been smashed in. It was a violent attack."

Becca paused as she digested this. Then she made him look at her. "Dalton, you tried your best today. If anything happens to her, it's not your fault. You aren't responsible for what this criminal does. He's the killer. Not you."

"But we were up there," Savage said, an edge to his voice. "We found

Candy's phone. If only we'd been better prepared." He shook his head. "It was too dark to carry on. Littleton was falling all over the place, it would have been madness to keep going."

"Exactly," she said. "You made the right call. Maybe you need to contact mountain rescue. They'd be better equipped to handle the search."

He snorted. "It'll take forever for Parks and Wildlife officials to get there, and even if they do, they can't search the entire mountain. No, we're going up again tomorrow morning, first thing."

Feeling strung out, he got up and pulled everything out of his backpack. As usual, Becca was right. What happened to that hiker and what might happen to Candy wasn't his fault, but he didn't feel any better about it. "Sorry if I'm grumpy. I'm tired, that's all. It's been a long day."

She nodded to his backpack. "Well, once you've done that, you'd better get some sleep. You're going to need it."

He loved that she didn't fuss. Nothing was going to stop him from going back up the mountain tomorrow, and she knew it. She knew him. He wasn't going to change anytime soon.

Once he'd repacked for the next day's excursion, he had a long, hot shower, then climbed into bed beside her. The lamp was off, and her steady, rhythmic breathing told him she was asleep. The same blissful oblivion didn't consume him, however, and he lay there for a long time, replaying events in his mind.

Where was Candy now? Was she alright? Was she alive? Were they already too late? Would Candy end up in the undergrowth just like the dead hiker?

He's the killer. Not you.

HIS ALARM WENT off at five AM, before the sun was even up. Groggy, Savage stumbled out of bed and pulled on his clothes.

Becca stirred. "Dalton?"

"Yeah?"

She reached for his hand. "Take care out there. I hope you find her."

"Thanks." He squeezed it, then bent over and kissed her warm forehead.

So do I.

He made a flask of coffee to go—it wasn't Jasmine's, but it would do—packed some supplies for the day's hike, threw in some extra ammo, and left the house just as the sky turned orange in the east.

The plan was to meet at the trailhead parking lot and go from there, but he was early and wanted to swing past where Mark Stillwell's body had been found. He sent Sinclair a text, telling the team to meet him at the dumpsite, and set off.

The trailhead was deserted this time of morning. Half an hour later, he'd start seeing the early hikers heading for the ridge, making a day of it. Right now, it was still too dark to see without a flashlight. He used his LED headlamp to light the way. The birthday gift from Barbara a couple of months back was proving useful.

The trail was silent, apart from the squawk of an eagle hunting for breakfast and the crunch of his boots on the gravel path. The air was fresh, biting into his face, making his eyes water.

He reached the first junction, then turned left, preparing for the steep elevation. His calves burned as he pushed on, taking deep breaths of fragrant mountain air. He could smell the pines and the aspens, along with the pungent scent of wildflowers and dust from the trail.

Eventually, the path leveled off and he paused, gazing out over the waking town of Hawk's Landing. It twinkled in the valley. Starlight glinted in the windows as the inhabitants rose to start their day. Beyond the town, over the distant purple hills, the sun came slowly to life. Still a subdued orange glow, it seemed to be psyching itself up for the day ahead.

Kinda like him.

After a drink from his water bottle, he continued along the contour path, careful not to lose his footing. Pines and oaks grew on either side of the trail, impeding the view, getting thicker as the trail progressed. Sections were scattered with loose rocks and pebbles that had fallen from above.

He enjoyed the hike and the solitude, even though his gut twisted every time he thought of Candy out here at the mercy of Jesse Turner. Had she made it through the night?

He felt a warmth on his back and turned around. The sun had made it over the hills, and was now heating the entire valley, including the south-facing slopes of the mountain. He closed his eyes and basked in the warmth for a moment, as if drawing energy from it. It felt good to shake off the predawn chill.

Another couple miles and he came to the edge of the national forest. The trees grew closer together, their branches entwining, clutching each other as if in a huddle. A gurgling reminded him the creek was nearby. Around the next bend, he saw it, rushing past, confined to its rocky banks. It was running full, thanks to the rains earlier in the week. Spruce and fir trees hugged the sides.

A slippery log had been placed over the gushing water. He traversed it, planting his feet firmly on the rounded bark, testing it first before putting his full weight on it. The last thing he needed was to end up in the water and spend the rest of the day in wet clothing.

Jumping down the other side, he checked the map upon which he'd scribbled the coordinates of Mark Stillwell's death. Almost there.

The path narrowed as the forest encroached and branches barred the way, as if to say, Keep Out. He pushed them aside and kept going until he saw the yellow markers. Police tape to the side of the path cordoned off the area where the body had been found. A garish reminder of the unnaturalness of what had occurred here.

He inched his way through the brush, glad he'd worn combat pants. The ground sloped sharply on this side of the track, and the earth beneath his boots felt soft and muddy.

He bent down and searched the area around where the body had been found, looking for a weapon or anything that might serve as a clue. Sure, the CSI team had done the same thing the night before, but visibility had been limited, and the harsh spotlights could have blinded them rather than assisted. They might have missed something.

Twenty minutes later, he stood back up, stretching out his back.

Nothing. The killer must have taken the murder weapon with him. If Jesse had used the butt of his revolver, then it made sense that it wouldn't be here.

Grimacing, he twisted his spine to iron out a kink when the clump of soil underneath him gave way. He slid a couple of feet down the embankment, grasping at low-lying branches to stabilize himself. It wasn't good enough. The soil was too muddy.

He lost his grip and tumbled a couple feet, hitting his knee on a rock. Growling an expletive, he dug in his boots and grasped anything he could find with his hands, until he came to a stop. Panting, he inspected his knee. It was bleeding and starting to swell, but nothing debilitating. Glancing up, he looked for the rock.

It was about the size of his shoe, and roughly the same shape. Long and rough. It protruded out of the ground, as if it had recently tumbled down the hill.

Was that mud on the surface?

Crawling up, he inspected it. No, it looked more like blood, and too much to be his.

His pulse ticked up a notch as he drew a glove out of his pack and picked up the rock. The beam from his headlamp illuminated the jagged edges soiled with the thick, sticky substance. Definitely blood.

He placed it in an evidence bag and laid it carefully at the top of his backpack. Then he crawled to the top of the embankment, scrambling on his hands and feet until he reached the dumpsite.

His knee was stinging, but he couldn't help feeling elated. He'd just found the murder weapon.

ELEVEN

THE SUN WAS JUST PEEKING out from behind the distant mountain range when Savage reached the rendezvous point.

Sinclair gasped when she saw him. "Boss, where have you been? We were getting worried." The fall and subsequent discovery had put him behind schedule.

"Slight detour." He dusted himself off. "I wanted to take another look at Stillwell's crime scene."

Thorpe eyed Savage's muddied pants and bloody knee. "Did you fall?"

"Yeah, the ground slid out from under me, but it turned out to be fortuitous. I found something."

They stared at him.

He switched off his headlamp—it wasn't needed now the sun was out—and shrugged off his backpack. As he bent over, a leaf fell out of his hair. Reaching inside, he pulled out the evidence bag. Handing it to Sinclair, he said, "I may have found the murder weapon."

She inspected it through the bag, pressing down on the sharp edges. "Is that blood?"

"Looks like it. That'll need to go to the lab."

"The killer hit Stillwell on the head with a giant rock?" Thorpe reasoned, his eyebrows rising above his glasses. "That's brutal."

"He was angry." Savage pictured the scene in his head. "Jesse must have approached from behind, saw Stillwell with Candy, lost it, and attacked Stillwell with the rock."

"And Candy?" Sinclair asked. "What did he do with her?"

"She could have run," Littleton said, which is no doubt what he'd have done.

"It's a possibility," Savage agreed. "He'd have caught up to her, though."

"You don't think—" Sinclair paused, frowning.

"We haven't found another body." Savage rushed on. "I'm sure she's still alive." He looked at the evidence bag. "Someone needs to take this back. Sinclair?"

"Sure." She stepped forward.

"I can do it," Littleton offered. It was clear he wanted to get off the mountain.

Sinclair spread her arms and shrugged her shoulders.

"I'd like you to stay with us," Savage said to Littleton, after a moment's thought. "You need the experience." And there was no one he trusted more than Sinclair to get the bloodied rock to the lab.

Littleton's shoulders sank, but he nodded. Sinclair took the packet and placed it in her backpack. Then she fastened it on her back and gave a mock salute. "See you guys back at the station."

Once she'd set off, Savage turned to Thorpe and Littleton. "Let's head up to the ridge. Candy and her captor could be anywhere along the route, and beyond."

The deputies each gave an uncertain nod. The path was narrow, and they had to fight branches and overhanging trees as they walked. Savage went first, taking the brunt of it, but Littleton, who was last, kept getting hit in the face.

A mile later, the trees thinned out, and they were back on the exposed hiking track. Sunlight streamed down, dazzling them with its brightness. They stopped, screening their eyes, and enjoyed the warmth on their faces. Nobody complained at the sudden glare. It felt great after the forest's chill.

At the next trail junction, the path forked. A signpost pointing to the right said Duck Creek Trail, and the path descended several hundred feet, looping back to the trailhead in a clockwise direction. The left-hand track veered upwards along the south face toward Stony Ridge.

They went left. Their breathing became labored. Savage knew from the map that they'd climbed almost 400 feet in under a mile. Like last night, the ground was dry and uneven, and loose material made walking difficult. They took their time, inching their way towards the ridge.

An hour uphill in the baking sun took its toll, and they were wilting by the time they reached the ridge. Perspiration dripped off Savage's face, and down between his shoulder blades. Thorpe's glasses kept sliding down his nose, and Littleton looked like he was about to pass out. So far, there was no sign of Candy or her captor.

"Let's have a water break," Savage instructed, as they all collapsed on a couple of big boulders and took off their packs. His mouth was dry as hell and he could taste dirt.

"It's hard to believe Candy would have made it up here," Thorpe reasoned, after a long pull on his water bottle.

"If she were running from Jesse, she might," Savage said. But Thorpe had a point. It was hard going, and Candy would have been alone and terrified.

"He might have held her at gunpoint," Littleton said, which was also true. Jesse could have forced her up to the ridge to kill her. There were plenty of forests and canyons on the eastern side of the mountain, off the beaten track, and infrequently visited as they were more dangerous and less user-friendly. A perfect burial ground. The only way to get there was over the ridge.

The mid-afternoon sun hammered down on their heads. Wiping away the sweat, they had a snack and replenished their energy. They'd been on the trail for several hours now.

"No signal." Thorpe frowned as he checked his phone. "I want to know if the tech team in Durango got anything off Candy's phone."

"We might catch service around the other side of the ridge." Savage remembered hearing something about a cell mast on the east side of the mountain, although he wasn't sure how far the range extended.

"They're going to have to hack her device," Thorpe continued, almost talking to himself. "I don't have the equipment for that."

"We'll follow up on that when we can," Savage said. "Right now, we've got to keep going. Once we're on the other side of that overlook, we're in state forest again. If he's going to kill her, I'm guessing it'll be there."

They shrugged into their backpacks and started walking along the ridge. It offered panoramic views across the valley, the neighboring farmlands, the lower reaches of the mountain, and the distant hazy hills of the Animas range. It was a shame they weren't in the right frame of mind to enjoy it.

Behind the overlook, the rough terrain turned muddy, and grass and wildflowers sprung up, their tips dancing in the sudden breeze. It was more exposed on this side, less protected from the elements. When it rained, the clouds hit here first, dumping their load before extending over the ridge and dissipating. As a result, the eastern slopes were covered in thousands of acres of thick aspen forest and comprised several rugged canyons with fast-flowing rivers and creeks.

The trio squelched along the path, dwarfed by enormous poplars reaching for the sky. Within a hundred feet, they were surrounded. If they hadn't been following a trail, they'd have gotten lost.

"What is that sound?" Thorpe asked.

"Just the wind." Savage glanced up. What had started as a low-pitched wail now howled like a banshee, screeching through the branches high above them. He could barely see the sky, thanks to the green canopy and clouds rumbling in.

"Candy could be anywhere." Littleton peered amongst the pillar-like trunks into the deepening forest.

Savage got a sinking feeling. They'd have to split up, but without a sat nav or any kind of GPS, they'd have a hard time finding each other again. Perhaps Becca had been right, and they should have waited for the park rangers.

In the distance, the men heard a guttural yell, followed by a loud bang. Echoes followed.

Savage's head jerked up. "That was a gunshot."

"Where'd it come from?" Thorpe twisted his head back and forth like a homing beacon. The trees had distorted the sound, bouncing it around the forest.

"I think it came from up ahead." Savage drew his gun.

The others readied their weapons and proceeded through the forest. Leaving the trail, they stepped over exposed root systems, clumps of grass and wildflowers. Savage kept an eye out for any sign of movement, his senses hyper alert.

To the left, a branch cracked.

They spun around. Before they could react, a beast of a bear broke through a huddle of trees and charged at them.

TWELVE

THE GROWLING, charging beast fixated on Savage. Hair bristling, saliva frothing, it romped towards him like a monster out of a nightmare.

For a split second, nobody moved. They were frozen with horror.

Then Savage's brain kicked into gear. Aiming, he prepared to pull the trigger, knowing full well that even if he did, it wouldn't stop the charging animal in time. He'd need a twelve-gauge for that.

Littleton, standing a short distance away, gasped. To everyone's surprise, the bear snapped its head to the side, momentarily distracted, then changed course and made a beeline for the young deputy.

Savage adjusted his aim, but it was too late. The bear launched itself at Littleton, who did what he'd been taught when faced with an aggressive bear. He dropped flat on his stomach and tucked. Cupping his hands over his head, he protected his face and ears.

The bear caught Littleton's backpack, tossing Littleton over like a ragdoll. The second strike to the ribs caused the deputy to yell out in pain. Savage couldn't get a clear shot, so he holstered his gun and ran at the bear's shoulder first, knocking it off balance. Thorpe took the opportunity to drag Littleton away.

Angered by Savage's assault, the grizzly turned its attention to the attacker. Savage went for his weapon, but the bear smacked it out of his hand. Another powerful swipe knocked Savage backwards off his foot, landing him several feet away. Winded and dazed, he shook his head to clear it. The bear loped forward on all fours. Only one thought flew through Savage's mind.

Move.

He scooted back on his butt, trying to get out of reach of another swipe, but didn't quite manage. The bear began to rise.

Savage turned away in a desperate attempt to protect his face from the coming blow.

A volley of shots rang out, echoing through the forest.

Startled, the grizzly tore off in a different direction, disappearing into the shadows. Savage looked up to see Thorpe with his pistol at ear height. The rounds he'd fired into the air had scared the bear off.

Thank God.

Savage collapsed back onto the ground, shaking with adrenaline.

That was close.

THORPE BENT OVER LITTLETON. "How's he doing?" Savage asked, getting up off the ground.

"Not good." Thorpe lifted Littleton's shirt to show the deep lacerations from the bear's claw.

Savage cringed. That didn't look great. The wounds were deep, and blood was smeared over his side like a macabre finger painting.

"We need to get him to a doctor," Thorpe said.

Savage gave a grim nod. "I've got a first-aid kit. Let's patch him up and see if we can call for a medevac."

"No signal," Thorpe reminded him. To drive the point home, he took out his phone and raised it above his head. "Nothing."

Damn.

Savage dived into his pack for the medical kit and laid it on the ground. He took out disinfectant spray and applied it to the wound.

Littleton grimaced. He was losing blood at a slow but steady rate.

"Hang in there." Savage covered the wound with gauze and applied pressure. It wasn't enough to stem the bleeding, but it would help. Hopefully it would give them the extra time they needed to get help. "We'll get you to a hospital soon."

"How?" Thorpe's brow creased with worry. They were miles from civilization, up in the mountains with no cell signal, no backup, and no way of getting out of there other than on foot.

"If we can get back to the Duck Creek trail junction, we can get down into the valley and call for an ATV." The Duck Creek trail was aimed at beginner hikers and the track was wider and smoother than the Stony Ridge trail. An emergency team could get a couple ATVs up and drive Littleton out.

Littleton mumbled something, and they both glanced down.

"What's that?" Savage asked.

"Let's do it," came the rasping whisper. "I can make it."

"You sure? We'll have to support you between the two of us. Can you walk?"

He nodded, grimacing.

They couldn't take Littleton's bag with them, so Savage took out the essentials, including a couple transponder sticks and extra ammo, and stuffed it into his own, then heaved it onto his back. "Okay, let's get you up."

Hoisting Littleton to his feet, they each put an arm around his waist to support him. Damn, for a slender guy, he was heavy. "Good?"

A clenched nod.

The bandage Savage had applied wouldn't last for long. Already, he could see fresh blood staining the deputy's shirt. Savage set a fast pace as they half-dragged, half-carried Littleton through the forest towards the ridge uphill. By the time they reached the overhang, both Savage and Thorpe were breathing heavily.

There was no time to stop. Littleton was trying his best, but he was failing fast. Every now and then he'd drop his head and the dead weight would drag both his and Thorpe's shoulders down. The deputy was drifting in and out of consciousness.

Savage met Thorpe's gaze over Littleton's drooping head.

Time was running out.

They struggled down the steep elevation, sliding and stumbling over the loose stones. Several times, they fell backwards onto their butts, feeling Littleton's knees buckling as they did so. Eventually, they made it to the bottom.

Savage heaved a sigh of relief. They paused and propped the lanky deputy against a boulder as they drank from their water bottles and wiped the sweat out of their eyes. It was almost dark now. Hard to believe they'd been hiking since daybreak. Then again, the Stony Ridge trail was known as a difficult climb. Not for beginners, Mark Stillwell's website had warned.

Yet here they were.

The sun had set behind the mountain peaks while they were in the forest. Shadows loomed all around them. Over the town, a sliver of the crescent moon began to rise.

The cool night air dried their damp faces but did nothing to rouse Littleton, now mostly unconscious, his shirt drenched with blood.

Savage knelt down to take a look. "Gotta change out this bandage," he said, shrugging out of his backpack. "It's soaked all the way through."

Thorpe nodded, too exhausted to say anything.

Savage's shoulders ached, and his leg throbbed where he'd been hit by the bear, but he hadn't had time to look at it. Littleton was deteriorating fast.

"Any signal yet?" Savage asked, hoping against hope that there was.

"Nope." Thorpe's voice had a hollowness to it.

"Dammit. We need to get word out. He's got to get medical treatment soon. We don't have long."

"I'll go down a couple of hundred feet and try there," Thorpe suggested.

Savage gave a rough nod. What else could they do? "Yeah, do it. I'll re-bandage the wound and wait for you."

Thorpe took off at a slow jog, his mouth set in a grim line of determination.

Savage delved into his bag again for the medical kit. He took out a fresh wad of gauze and replaced the drenched one, pressing the edges down against Littleton's sticky skin. He'd hoped the bleeding would have stopped by now, but that didn't appear to be the case.

Taking out his water bottle, he put it to Littleton's lips. They were dry and parched. He barely swallowed, the water dripping down his chin.

"Hang in there, buddy," Savage told him. "We're almost there."

Littleton groaned in response.

At least he could hear them, even if he didn't have the energy to speak. Savage got himself ready and was about to pull Littleton up and continue down the path by himself when Thorpe came marching back.

"Got ahold of the emergency services," he said. "ETA is forty minutes."

Forty minutes. He hoped Littleton would make it that long.

What a disaster. It had taken them two hours to get back to the trail junction, all the while a crazy gun-wielding maniac still had Candy captive.

Savage gritted his teeth in frustration.

"I'll wait with him." Thorpe said.

"No, that's okay. He's my responsibility."

"So is Candy," Thorpe said. "You go back. I'll get Littleton to the paramedics and come back to find you."

Savage studied his colleague's dirty, drawn face with smudges over his glasses. They were all stretched to the limit. He couldn't ask much more of his team.

"If you're sure."

Thorpe nodded. "See you in a couple hours."

Savage patted Littleton on the shoulder, then set off back up the ridge.

THIRTEEN

BY THE TIME Savage got to the ridge, his thigh was aching. Perhaps he'd better take a look. He undid his pants and pulled them down, exposing a nasty scratch. It wasn't nearly as bad as Littleton's, but it was raw and seeping and needed cleaning.

Perching against a boulder, he got out the medical kit and sprayed his wound with disinfectant. Damn, that stung. While waiting for it to dry, he dug back in the kit for some gauze, but they'd used most of it on the deputy. He found a thin strip and a couple of band aids and secured those in place. It would have to do.

Pulling his pants back up, he looked across the view. Hawk's Landing lay nestled in the dark valley below. A sparkling strip of lights in the otherwise darkened crevice. It looked warm and welcoming, and very far away.

Up here, they were on the edge of the mountain. Behind him, he could feel the cold air move in, bringing with it a hint of rain. It prickled his neck and made the hairs stand up. Or was that an omen of the task ahead?

It was time to put on his protective waterproof jacket. It didn't have much insulation, but it would ward off the worst of the chill and keep him dry.

Sparing a last thought for Littleton, he headed over the ridge, towards the aspen forest on the other side. The giant trees loomed up ahead, the wood line dark and impenetrable. Clenching his jaw, he strode into the darkness. The giant poplars towered over him as if in a weird fantasy world. A world where bad things happened.

He found Littleton's backpack, and his blood on the ground.

Savage swallowed, refusing to think about what would happen if the grizzly came back. Gritting his teeth, he reached for his gun.

This is where they'd been when they'd heard someone yell, and then the gunshot. It had been a male voice, so not Candy. Was it Jesse? Had Candy somehow got the better of him? Was the parolee injured? He rubbed his forehead. What the hell was going on up here?

Savage ventured deeper into the forest, staying on what was left of the trail, assuming the shooter had done the same. Leaving the beaten track in this forest would have been fatal. He'd never find his way back.

Amongst the trees, it was pitch black. No moonlight penetrated from above, and without his headlamp and flashlight, he'd have stumbled around in the dark. Cold crept under his outer layer of clothing and seeped into his skin. Moisture clung to his neck and face, lowering his core body temperature.

The sounds of the night grew louder as creatures came out to prey. It would be foolish to keep going now. Besides, he was exhausted and his thigh was killing him.

A fire would ward off the cold and provide safety from wild animals, but he didn't want to risk it. The killer was out there somewhere, and a campfire would only serve as a beacon. It would be better to remain incognito and approach stealthily in the morning.

Thorpe had already given their position away by firing that shot to ward off the bear. The killer would have heard that and moved on, especially if he had Candy.

Savage took off his bag and laid it against a tree. There was no natural shelter, although the underbrush did provide a soft surface to sit on.

Damn, his leg hurt. He lay back against his backpack and stared up at the chaos of branches overhead, surreal in the light of his headlamp. Slowly, his eyes flickered closed.

GRASS TICKLED HIS NECK. The mattress beneath him was hard and cold.

Savage blinked open his weary eyes. Then it all came flooding back. The trail. The gunshot. The bear. Littleton. Candy.

He sat up.

Was that rustling in the bushes behind him? Reaching for his gun, he spun around, heart thudding. Not the bear. Not again. Or was it something worse? Someone worse?

The undergrowth moved. The leaves swayed. His finger tightened on the trigger.

A raccoon scurried out of the grass, dark eyes cautious in its white furry face. A second later, another raccoon joined, casting furtive glances his way. Savage sat very still, trying not to startle them.

The grass rustled again, and a baby raccoon poked its head out. Ignoring Savage, it scampered over to its parents.

Savage relaxed.

As the raccoon family disappeared, his thoughts turned to his unborn child. What was he doing out here on the side of the mountain when he should be at home with his fiancé?

Candy.

She needed his help. No one else was coming for her. And even he might be too late.

Grimacing, he got to his feet and dusted himself off. Thinking like that wouldn't get him anywhere. Becca's words came back to him.

If she's still alive, you'll find her. After a quick snack and some water, he set off again, wincing at the soreness in his leg. It was stiffer than yesterday, but that was expected. He kept going, moving his arms around to ward off the early dawn chill. The sun hadn't penetrated the forest yet, and it was several degrees colder within the foliage.

A low cloud had moved in, and an early morning mist permeated the green canopy above, adding a surrealness to the environment. A noise up ahead gave him pause. What the hell was that? A whiny, whimpering murmur. Could it be the plaintive cries of a wounded animal?

He slunk forward, careful to not make a sound, his gun at the ready. Before he could round on it, he spun around at the loud crash behind him.

"Oh, thank goodness. It's you."

Thorpe.

God only knew what time he must have set off this morning. Savage grinned with gratitude. The nerdy deputy, more comfortable in front of a computer, had leaves stuck to his fleece and a branch sticking out of his backpack. His glasses were askew, and he looked like he'd been fighting his way through the brush all night—which, in fact, he probably had.

Thorpe opened his mouth to speak, but Savage held a finger to his lips. The deputy fell silent. Savage pointed through the trees. Thorpe drew his weapon and crept beside the Sheriff.

There it was again. A whimper, followed by a plaintive moan. Savage's hair stood on end.

"What's that?" whispered Thorpe, his eyes huge.

They inched around the trees towards the sound. A weak sunlight worked hard to dissipate the mist, casting an eerie glow on the ground where a patch of earth had been dug up.

"Looks like a shallow grave." Savage's voice was hoarse.

Thorpe gulped.

Savage glanced around the small clearing, but the plot was empty. Only the overhead trees looked down on them as they approached.

"Is it her?" Thorpe asked.

Savage moved forward. They'd find out soon enough.

Another cry and Thorpe jumped back. "Jeez, it's alive!"

A pale, zombie-like hand rose out of the soil.

What the–?

For a split-second, they both stared in horror, then rushed forward to help. Dropping to their knees, they pawed at the soil, digging out whomever lay buried there. Was it Candy?

As the soil went flying, Savage muttered an expletive. He recognized the victim.

Jesse Turner.

Bloody, dirty, and pale as the undead, they lifted him out. He was alive, but barely. There was a gaping wound in his head, evidence of massive trauma. His scalp glistened despite the dirt, and his eyes rolled back in his head.

They set him down on the ground. Shaken, Thorpe glanced at Savage, who gave a tiny shake of his head.

He wouldn't last long. His injuries were too severe. There was nothing they could do to save Jesse Turner.

FOURTEEN

"WHERE'S CANDY?" Savage asked, as they laid Jesse on the ground.

Glazed eyes stared up at them. The man was barely conscious.

"Jesse, can you hear me?" Savage waved a hand in front of his face. "What happened? Where's Candy? What have you done to her? Is she alive?"

Or had he already killed her? Had she done this to him in a bid for freedom? Was she racing through the forest, alone and afraid?

His eyelids flickered and for a moment, Jesse held a defiant gaze. "I didn't... I didn't do anything to her." He faded off, unable to get the words out.

The sky was lightening, but they remained in shadow.

"Where is she?" Savage asked.

A small shake of the head. "I—" He swallowed the words, then coughed up blood. It dribbled out of the corner of his mouth, mingling with the dirt and grime on his face. "I—I tried to save her."

Savage thought he'd misheard. "What?"

No response. Jesse had lost consciousness. Savage felt for a pulse, it was faint and erratic. The fugitive didn't have long. The Sheriff sucked in a breath, then let it out in a frustrated rush. They needed answers.

"Jesse, can you tell us what happened?" He gave the injured man a little shake.

"He. Took. Candy." The words were an effort.

"He?" Thorpe shot Savage a puzzled glance. "Who?"

Savage shrugged and shook his head. He glanced back down at Jesse. Jesse Turner had been their primary suspect. He'd gone after Candy with the intent to harm her, and now he was the one lying in a ditch.

"The head wound is similar to Mark Stillwell's," Thorpe muttered.

Savage gave a grim nod. That fact hadn't escaped him. "Heavy object. Blunt force trauma." It could have been a rock, or the butt of a revolver. He looked around and saw no obvious murder weapon. No bloodied stone. No gun.

Savage resisted the urge to shake him awake. "Who's he? Who took Candy?"

Jesse's eyes had closed again, his face getting paler by the second. Savage put a hand on the injured man's shoulder and felt him flinch. It was subtle. Even when he was dying, he didn't want a lawman to touch him.

Removing his hand, Savage bent over so his face was inches from the dying man's. "Jesse? Jesse, you've got to tell us who did this. Who's got Candy?"

A small shake of the head. "I—I don't know."

Damn.

Savage grit his jaw. What the hell was going on? Why was their main suspect lying here with a hole in his head? Where was Candy?

Judging by the head wound, Jesse had been here for at least twelve hours, from about the time they'd dealt with the black bear.

Th e shot.

The one they'd heard before the grizzly appeared out of the trees and derailed their search.

He glanced back at the shallow grave. "Jesse's brother said he took his gun. Where is it?"

Thorpe's head snapped up, his eyes registering. "I'll take a look." He sifted through the upturned soil, clawing at it like a dog. A moment later, he glanced up. "It's not here."

"Did you use your weapon?" Savage asked. "Jesse, look at me. Did you fire your weapon?"

A grunt.

"Did you hurt Candy?"

His eyes fluttered open. "No. Would...never...hurt...Candy."

Savage exhaled. Thank God, she was still alive. But then... "Who did you shoot?"

"Him. He took her. I—I got a shot off. Think I hit him." Jesse's head rolled to the side. More blood ran out of the corner of his mouth.

"Where did they go?" Savage clutched the fugitive's shoulder.

No response.

"Jesse, help us. Help us find Candy."

Jesse made one last attempt to open his eyes, but instead of looking at Savage, he stared up at the trees. He seemed incapable of controlling his eye movement. His system was shutting down.

"Do you know where they went?" Savage tried one last time. They watched on as Jesse's life ebbed out of him.

The fugitive lifted his hand and pointed east.

"East. They went that way?" Savage asked.

A nod.

Savage glanced at Thorpe, who was staring at Jesse, biting his lip. He knew the end was coming.

The hand flopped back down on the cold, hard ground. As the sun broke through the trees and warmed the back of their heads, Jesse took a final shuddering breath, and closed his eyes for the last time.

"IF JESSE DIDN'T KILL Mark Stillwell, or kidnap Candy, there's someone else out here." Savage moved away from Jesse. The fugitive lay motionless in front of them, his face a mixture of dirt and blood, the gaping wound on his head glistening in the early morning sunlight. "How did we get it so wrong?"

"We couldn't have known." Thorpe ran a sleeve over his face. He looked shattered. Unshaven, dark shadows beneath his eyes, leaves sticking to his clothing. Savage supposed he looked much the same. Except they were nowhere near to solving this. There was more to do.

"He said he got off a shot," Thorpe pointed out.

"Maybe our guy is wounded." Savage gazed through the trees, hands on his hips. "That will make him easier to track."

Thorpe stood up, nodding. "What should we do with Jesse?"

"We'll have to leave him here for now." Savage checked his phone. Still no reception. "Once we're further east, we should be able to pick up a signal."

Thorpe placed a transponder beside the body. There was no time to bury him properly. They had to find Candy. If she was with an unidentified killer, then time was running out. The monster had already killed two grown men. God only knew what he was doing to her. It didn't bear thinking of.

"Let's get going."

Thorpe dusted himself off, gave Jesse one last look, then turned away. "Right behind you."

FIFTEEN

CANDY STAGGERED AHEAD of her captor. Hot tears streamed down her face. Jesse was dead. The man she'd thought she'd loved once. Before he'd gotten involved with Lick and his gang of losers. Before she'd turned him in.

The tears made it hard to see where she was going. She tripped and fell to the ground, grazing her knee.

"Get up!" Walker ordered, prodding her with a long stick like she was an animal. Gritting her teeth, she pushed herself off the ground. It stung, but she hardly felt it. Grief numbed her. She swallowed over the foul taste in her mouth.

Jesse had come looking for her. All those letters he'd sent her, the ones she hadn't read. The ones she had. He'd been trying to get her attention. He'd always loved her, she knew that. The problem was, she hadn't loved him back. Not the way he'd wanted. Then she'd sold him out. What choice did she have? Dealing drugs and holding up convenience stores. It hadn't sat right with her. Despite her upbringing, or perhaps in spite of it, she had a strong sense of right and wrong.

She'd turned a blind eye to Jesse's antics until he'd injured an old man in a convenience store. That had been the last straw. She'd gone to the sheriff and told her side of the story. Agreed to testify. Jesse had been sentenced to three years—she felt bad about that. He deserved to serve time for his crime, but he didn't deserve to be beaten to death.

Shutting her eyes didn't help. The visuals stuck with her. Walker picking up the rock. Jesse's first shot going wild. The second hitting Walker in the shoulder. He'd barely flinched before reaching Jesse and bringing the rock down on his head. Over and over and over again.

He'd beaten Jesse until his head was a bloody mess. At first Jesse had cried out, tried to fight him off. But Walker was bigger and stronger, and fueled by rage. The yells had changed to groans. Jesse lay motionless. Then, even the groaning had stopped.

That's when she knew he was dead. The one person who'd cared enough to come looking for her was now buried in a shallow ditch a mile behind her.

The man was inhuman. A monster. Bile rose in her throat and she gagged, but she managed not to puke.

"Keep going," Walker barked, waving Jesse's revolver at her. He turned around to peer into the shadows behind them. Last night, after Jesse had been killed, they'd heard a gunshot from deep within the forest. Probably just hunters. Out of desperation, she'd called out, but Walker had slapped her face and stuffed a dirty gag into her mouth. Later, he'd taken it out to give her some water. "Scream again and I'll kill you."

She believed him.

He was on edge, she could tell. Paranoid. Convinced there was someone behind them, following them.

If only...

Surrounded by trees, she felt like they were the only two people left on the planet. Not a nice feeling when one is a killer.

The wound in Walker's shoulder gave him some discomfort now. He grunted with every step.

Good.

She'd noticed him wincing, his face drawn, his lips pulled back in a permanent grimace. The bullet had grazed his arm, leaving a bloody gash, but as far as she could tell, it wasn't stuck inside. Blood stained his T-shirt, seeping into the fabric. If it wasn't treated, it would fester, causing an infection. She hoped it damn well killed him.

"Why don't you just shoot me?" she spat, after he'd prodded her in the back yet again. "Why take me with you? I'm only slowing you down." Exhaustion and fear made her reckless.

He didn't respond.

"Where are we going, anyway?"

She'd had enough. Her feet were killing her, she was scratched and bruised, and sick of being treated like an animal. If he was planning to kill her, she wanted to know.

"I'm going to take my time with you." He leered at her. "As soon as we get out of the mountains and into the valley. I know a place."

He left it hanging.

Her pulse raced. Fear clutched at her chest, making it hard to breathe. That didn't give her much time. Back in high school, she'd been cornered by a bully underneath the bleachers. He'd pushed her to the ground and jumped on top of her. She still remembered how he smelled of sweat mixed with freshly cut grass. Whatever he'd thought of doing, he'd changed his mind after she'd kicked him in the nuts with such force, he'd taken a full week off school.

That was only part of what was coming Walker's way. But first, she had to get him to let his guard down.

"What place?" she asked.

He fed off her fear, she could tell. A smirk crossed his face. "A cabin. It belonged to someone I—" He paused. "Used to know."

Someone he'd murdered, he meant. She shivered, kicking herself for getting abducted in the first place. How could she have been so naïve?

He'd seemed so friendly, with an easy smile and striking blue eyes. After her hurried exit from Hawk's Landing, she was grateful for the company, and it didn't hurt that he was easy on the eyes. He'd asked how come she was hiking alone. She'd given him a vague story, just enough truth to be believable. Getting away for a while. Taking some time out to think about things. It was complicated.

He'd assumed it was boyfriend trouble, and she hadn't corrected him.

Walker wasn't the first person she'd met that day. Earlier, she'd met a guy named Mark. They'd sat together for a while, admiring the view and talking about where they'd grown up. He was from Colorado Springs and worked for a tourism company. They'd even taken a selfie together before saying goodbye. She wondered what had happened to him. Her gut twisted. Had Walker killed him too?

It was when she'd been talking to Walker that she'd first noticed the backpack. It closely resembled the one Mark had worn. At first, she'd thought it a coincidence. After all, the outdoor stores all stocked the same brands. But she had seen the *I love Colorado Springs* keyring attached to the zipper.

Mark had one just like it.

A chill had shot down her spine. Confused, she'd asked Walker where he was from, and he'd said out of town. "Not Colorado Springs, then?"

He glanced at her, then over his shoulder at the keyring.

"Oh, that." A laugh that didn't meet his eyes. "That was a souvenir I picked up last week."

Nah. She wasn't buying it. Walker had stolen Mark's backpack. The knowledge unsettled her. So much so, she'd tried to get away from him, pretending to sprain her ankle so he'd go on ahead. That's when Jesse had found them.

Jesse.

Why hadn't he stayed in the valley and just got on with his life? Forgotten about her? He'd still be alive now.

She closed her eyes. Those images again.

She gritted her teeth in determination. Walker was a bully. Worse, he was a bully with a gun. Still, he was gonna pay. For what he'd done to Jesse and—she suspected—also to Mark.

She just had to find a way. A moment of weakness.

They walked on, across the uneven ground riddled with roots and clumps of bushes. Walker was wheezing now, his T-shirt drenched with blood. Their pace had slowed. The arm holding the gun—the arm that was injured—hung uselessly at his side. That should give her an advantage.

Maybe it was time to make her move.

SIXTEEN

SAVAGE AND THORPE left Jesse Turner's body in the ditch and hiked on. Once they got back, they'd send a mountain rescue team to retrieve him.

"Looks like rain," Savage said. The sky was an ominous grey, and a low mist had moved in, snaking around their feet. It seeped between the trees like a scene from a horror movie.

"As if this place wasn't spooky enough." Thorpe pulled his jacket closer around him. It was filthy, and Savage felt a surge of gratitude to the deputy who'd hiked most of the night to get back to him and help search for Candy.

"Did the techies manage to get anything off Candy's phone?" Savage asked.

"No, they haven't hacked it yet. I don't know if they ever will, to be honest. I have some friends who might be able to, but I can't do anything until I get back.

"We don't even know if we're on the right track." Savage rubbed his eyes. The lack of sleep and chilly conditions were getting them both down. He thought once again of his warm bed back in Hawk's Landing, his fiancé curled up in it, and questioned what the hell he was doing out here.

Candy. The thought gave him a much-needed shot of adrenaline.

"Jesse said they headed east." Thorpe gestured in that direction.

"Let's get going," Savage said. The forest covered half the mountain. They had a lot of ground to cover.

They headed downhill, the elevation steeper the further they went. The ground turned muddy and their boots fought for traction. When the trees parted, the carpet of green extended as far as the eye could see. There were no twinkling lights here, no town nestling in the valley. This was uninhabitable land, an inhospitable mix of forest and brush, veined with creeks and rivers soaking the ground. Even hiking off the trail was hazardous.

They trudged on, forced to slow down. Had Candy and her captor come this way? It was hard to tell. Savage clenched his jaw in frustration.

Thorpe let out a yell. Savage spun around to see his deputy sliding several feet down the hill, his hands grasping at plants and trees to steady himself. Finally, he came to a gurgling halt.

"You okay?" Savage called.

Thorpe, embarrassed, wiped his hands on his pants. "I think I landed in a puddle."

Savage sidled over to him, careful not to lose his own footing. Looking down at where Thorpe was standing, he said, "I don't think that's just a puddle of water. There's blood mixed in that." There were two light red smears on Thorpe's pants. "That's blood."

"Oh, crap!" Thorpe stared down in horror. Sure enough, his legs were covered in watery, sticky blood.

"Must be the killer's." Savage crouched down to take a closer look.

Thorpe got to his feet and moved out of the puddle, trying to control his breathing. The blood had shocked him.

Savage surveyed the ground. "It could be from that bullet wound."

"Jesse was right," murmured Thorpe. He poured a little of his drinking water on his hands and rubbed them together to clean them.

There was nothing he could do about his stained pants. "He did hit the guy."

"That'll slow him down." Savage stood and peered through the trees.

"And give us something to track." Thorpe looked ahead for more blood spatter, although it was hard to make out in the dim light. The frequent rainfall on this part of the mountain created lots of wet patches.

They switched on their flashlights to see the blood markings more easily. They moved on, eyes peeled for the crimson stains to lead them in the direction of Candy and her abductor.

"She's likely still alive," Savage murmured, working his flashlight in an arc in front of him.

"He'll need to stop and see to his wound." Thorpe pointed to more blood spatter. "It looks like he's bleeding profusely."

"That's when we'll strike," Savage whispered, keeping his voice down. They must be getting close and noise carried in the close confines of the forest.

They needed the element of surprise. With the killer injured, and two of them in pursuit, the odds were in their favor.

Hang on, Candy. We're coming.

―――――

CANDY WATCHED AS WALKER STUMBLED, then righted himself. He scowled at her. "What are you looking at?"

"You're injured," she muttered. "Maybe we should stop for a while."

"We're not stopping."

"I could treat your wound," she said. "It's bleeding a lot."

"It's fine," he barked, shrugging it off.

"I know how to treat a gunshot wound. Stitch you up good."

His eyes slanted. "How'd you learn to do that?"

"Growing up around these parts, you learn stuff." She shrugged. Everyone who'd lived in the trailer park owned a gun. She'd grown up around them. She was a pretty good shot, too, although she hadn't practiced in a while.

He grunted, but prodded her with the stick again. They weren't stopping yet. "Could you at least untie me?" she asked. "I'm not going anywhere up here. My hands are turning numb."

"Shut up and keep moving." Another prod.

Damn.

She'd have to get him to untie her if she was going to make a run for it. Patience, she told herself. Have patience. He'd have to stop eventually.

A drizzle of rain pricked her face, and she glanced up. Voluminous gray clouds circled ahead, just beyond the tops of the trees. It was misty too, the kind of dampness that seeped into your clothing and gave you the chills. The air had that familiar dank smell, like a wet cloth over your face. There was a rainstorm coming.

That meant they'd have to take shelter. Visibility would be low. The ground treacherous.

Patience.

Walker stumbled again. This time he stopped, clutching his arm. "Ugh," he gritted.

"You're in pain." She turned around. "Let's take a break. I swear, I know what I'm doing."

He regarded her suspiciously.

"If you don't," she said, "it will become infected, and you don't want that. Not out here." She waved an arm around. There was nothing but trees and underbrush for miles.

A large raindrop landed on her nose. Any moment now.

Walker glanced up. "Keep going," he rasped.

Heart sinking, she walked on. The rain got heavier, and soon it was pelting down on them. Tiny daggers prickled her skin. Walker huffed and puffed behind her, clearly in pain. He'd switched the gun to his left hand—she'd seen him use his right to pummel Jesse. This was good. He'd be less effective now, less accurate.

They rounded an overhang, and she spotted a cave under the craggy outcrop. "What about there?" she blurted out, pointing to it. "We can shelter and wait out the storm."

Walker grunted in reply. He didn't have the energy to talk anymore. Good. He was weakening fast.

Water poured off their faces and backpacks, dribbling down their arms and legs, soaking their shoes and socks. Without waiting for a reply, Candy headed to the outcrop. For once, Walker didn't argue.

Out of the deluge, he shrugged off his backpack and collapsed on the ground. His face was pale and pinched. She knelt in front of him and held out her wrists. "Untie me and I'll help you."

He frowned.

"That wound needs a bandage before it gets infected," she stressed.

Walker gestured to the backpack. "I'll get it."

She gritted her teeth as he looked inside. It wasn't even his bag, it was Mark's. Mark with the kind face and crinkly eyes. She'd liked him. Was he lying in a ditch, too? A shiver passed over her.

Breathe. Wait for the right moment.

He took out the medical kit and rummaged for the disinfectant and a bandage. Grimacing, he peeled off his T-shirt, exposing the raw striation where the bullet had grazed him. It was deep, but not fatal. With the bandage, he'd live, as long as it didn't get infected. He was well built, the muscles toned. Muscles used to smash Jesse's head in.

She bit her lip. *Keep it together.*

It was pouring down now, the rain splashing off the ground creating mini craters outside the cave. He wasn't going anywhere.

He smeared disinfectant over the wound, cringing. Then he stripped off the back of the bandage and handed it to her. Hands bound, she applied it to the wound, with a little more force than necessary.

"We need a fire," he rasped, falling back against his bag.

"I can do that."

She needed a distraction if she was going to escape. Needed to lull him into a false sense of security. He'd lost a lot of blood, and she could tell he was woozy. He'd recover after some food and rest, so she had a very small window of opportunity.

The cave was empty, except for a few thick logs, a pile of dead leaves, and a twisted bush to one side near the entrance with branches sticking out in all directions. More importantly, the branches were dry. She pulled as many off as she could, then made a fire. The dead leaves would act as kindling.

"I need more wood." She turned to him. "I'll go and see what I can find that isn't too wet."

He raised the revolver. "You'll stay here and use what you've got. That'll do."

Sighing, she gave a small nod. It had been worth a shot.

She took some matches out of his bag and lit the fire, cupping her hands so the spark would take. After several unsuccessful attempts, it caught alight.

Walker watched all this with guarded eyes, gun still pointed at her. "Sit down. Take off your shoes."

"What?"

"Take off your goddamn shoes."

"Okay, okay." She positioned her backpack against the wall and leaned against it. Slowly, she undid her laces and took off her tennis shoes.

"And your socks."

"Really?"

He gave her a look. Reluctantly, she peeled off her sodden socks. The ground was uneven. A blanket of leaves and shrubs covered sticks and stones. Barefoot, her escape would be a lot more difficult.

Heat from the fire drifted over, warming her skin and drying her clothes. It crackled while the rain poured down outside. Under any normal conditions, she'd have enjoyed this moment.

She picked up a fat log with both hands and stoked the fire, trying to keep it going.

Walker's shoulders dropped, and the hand holding the gun lowered. His eyelids flickered, as he fought to stay awake.

Come on. Candy gripped the stick. *Fall asleep.*

He was losing the battle. His eyelids drooped and his gun hand dropped.

Now.

Candy raised the burning log and holding it with both hands, she smashed it across Walker's head.

He fell to the side, screaming and clutching his head. Candy didn't wait to see what happened next. She leaped to her feet, hands still bound, and took off into the driving rain.

SEVENTEEN

SAVAGE HELD UP A HAND. Thorpe came to a halt beside him. "What?"

"I think we're close. Can you smell that?"

The deputy sniffed the air. His glasses had steamed up. How he could see anything through them, Savage had no idea.

"Smoke?" Thorpe asked. It was faint, but discernible, wafting through the trees.

"What do you bet our killer has taken shelter from the rain and made a fire?" Savage asked, swiping water from his eyes. They were both drenched.

Thorpe gave a sharp nod. "Just like we hoped."

The terrain had been changing for the last half mile or so. The thick forest had given way to a sparser jumble of vegetation. Low-lying shrubs and bushes clawed at their knees, while pines and firs poked their heads out above them, but it wasn't as dense as before. They had to camouflage themselves.

Thorpe checked his phone, then gave an excited gasp. "I've got signal."

"Seriously?"

"Yeah." He held up his phone, sheltering it with his other hand. One definite bar flickered to two as Thorpe lifted his arm, then went back down to one as he lowered it.

"Call Sinclair." A surge of adrenaline shot through Savage. "Tell her to get a chopper up here. We'll need a way off this mountain once we find Candy." It would take too long on foot, and they had no idea what condition she would be in. Given their own state, hers wouldn't be good. She'd been on the mountain far longer than they had, and at the mercy of a cold-blooded killer.

"Will a helicopter fly in this?" Thorpe asked, as rain dripped off the rim of his glasses onto his nose.

Savage scowled. "Let's hope so."

The smell of smoke grew stronger every time the wind blew their way. They didn't have a visual yet, but the campers couldn't be far off.

Thorpe made the call, sheltering under an oak tree. He turned the volume down, but put it on speaker, so Savage could hear. They huddled together, waiting for her to answer.

"Holy crap, Thorpe!" Sinclair exclaimed, her relief evident. "Where are you guys? We've been trying to reach you."

"We're on the east side of the mountain," Thorpe replied.

"Where? I can't hear you."

Thorpe raised his voice, repeating their location. Savage made a frantic hand signal to keep it down.

Thorpe grimaced and lowered it again. "I can't speak any louder. We need an evac. Can you send a helicopter?"

Her voice kept fading in and out. "You need a chopper?"

"Yeah." He shifted to the side, away from the tree.

"Okay, I'll see what I can do. The State Patrol must have one."

The connection improved. Savage put his head close to the phone. "Tell them to hurry. We're in pursuit of the suspect."

"You are?"

"Yeah, we're closing in," Thorpe replied.

"And Candy?" Sinclair's voice was hesitant. "Is she alive?"

"We think so," Savage said.

"Oh, thank goodness." They heard Sinclair relay the message to Barbara.

"I'm on it," she said, coming back on the line. "Text me your coordinates or drop a pin so I know where to send them."

"Will do," Thorpe replied. "There's a clearing here, where the helicopter can land."

"I only hope they'll fly in this weather," she said.

"See what you can do." Savage cut in. They were about to hang up when Sinclair said, "I almost forgot. You know that blood on the rock you found near Mark Stillwell?"

"Yeah?"

"It wasn't his."

"No?" Savage frowned. If it didn't belong to the victim, it must have belonged to the killer. His pulse escalated. "The attacker must have cut his hand when he was hitting the victim."

"It wasn't Jesse Turner's either," Sinclair said, excitement in her voice.

Savage had forgotten she wasn't aware there was another perpetrator on the trail. "We know."

A pause. "Wait, how do you know that?"

"We found Jesse. He'd been beaten to death, just like Mark Stillwell."

There was a long silence. "So, this killer's murdered two people?"

"Looks that way."

They heard her exhale. Barbara may have said something along the lines of, "Sweet Jesus," but Savage couldn't be sure.

"Do we know whose blood it is?" Savage asked.

Her voice was shaky. "The name in the police database was Ernest Dixon, aged 32. He's wanted in connection with the disappearance of a 20-year-old woman in New Mexico."

That was potentially three people he'd killed—that they knew of. Who's to say there weren't more? Savage shivered, and it had nothing to do with the rain.

"Ernest Dixon," he repeated, glancing at Thorpe. They finally had a name for their killer.

After they'd hung up, Thorpe looked at Savage. "What should we do now, boss?"

The rain wouldn't last forever. Right now, their suspect was taking shelter, injured and bleeding. Once the rain stopped, he'd move on. Besides, a helicopter would give away their position. They'd need it for an evac, but Savage's gut was telling him now was their moment.

"Let's keep going," he said. "You ready?"

Thorpe took out his service pistol and checked it.

Then he glanced up. "Ready."

EIGHTEEN

CANDY RACED barefoot through the dark forest, ignoring the twigs and sharp pebbles digging into her feet. Her only thought was that she needed to get as far away from Walker as possible. The rain-covered ground made her fall, grazing her knees and covering herself in mud.

None of it mattered.

The blow to Walker's head wouldn't last long. At this point, he was probably shaking it off and coming after her. She zigzagged through the trees, going in no particular direction. Perhaps she could confuse him, make him realize following her would be futile. She trekked downhill, hoping to reach the outskirts of a small community, or a road where she might flag down a driver. The trail had long since vanished, as they were miles from civilization.

A rustling behind her caused her to speed up. Was that him? Had he gained on her? She sprinted on, half-expecting a bullet to fly past, if not embed itself in her back. She wouldn't put it past him to kill her in cold blood.

The light was dull and gray, and the pouring rain limited visibility to a few feet. That was a good thing. She scrambled on, falling again, picking herself up, surging forward. Her breath came in loud gasps, but she tried to subdue it for fear of being heard.

Trees loomed out of nowhere, and she skidded around them, losing herself amongst the leaves. Large boulders lay up ahead, fallen from the peaks above. She darted through them, raindrops streaming into her eyes.

Bam!

It was like hitting a brick wall. She gasped and fell onto her butt. Looking up, she realized it wasn't a wall, but a man. He was standing right over her, holding a gun.

"I'm sorry," she wailed, squeezing her eyes shut. At any moment, the blast would tear straight through her head, shattering her brain. Lights out. This is what it had come to. She'd die here in the mountains, her body never to be found.

Would he bury her in a shallow grave, like he had Jesse? She stifled a sob.

"I didn't mean to run away. Please, don't shoot. I don't want to die."

"You're not going to die."

She opened her eyes. "Huh?" That wasn't Walker's voice.

Cargo pants, not hiking shorts. A waterproof jacket, not a T-shirt. No bullet wound. Too tall to be Walker.

Thank you, God.

She fell forward like a rag doll as the tension left her body.

The man holstered his gun and offered her a hand. "Here, let me help you."

She took his hand with both of hers and he pulled her to her feet. She winced, noticing the pain for the first time. "Who are you?"

"I'm Sheriff Savage from Hawk's Landing. We've met before, long time ago. This is Deputy Thorpe."

Thorpe nodded at her. "Ma'am."

Savage gripped her hands. "You're safe now."

She sank against him and burst into tears. It wasn't like her to cry, but she couldn't help it. The relief was so intense. His arm went around her back and he held her steady until the shock wore off. Eventually, she broke away.

"I'm sorry." She tried to rub her eyes, but her hands were still bound. "There's this guy, Walker, he kidnapped me and, and—" She paused to gather her thoughts. She was rambling on like an idiot, and to the Sheriff no less. Her people didn't usually associate with the law, let alone hug them. Embarrassed, she took a step back and tried to compose herself.

"We know about the man who kidnapped you," the Sheriff said. He had a kind, craggy face, softened by hazel eyes. His gaze fell to her wrists. "Lift up your hands."

She held them out, watching as he cut through the bindings with a hunting knife. Blood rushed back into her hands, burning. She rubbed them together to get the circulation going.

"Did you say we'd met before?" His words had only just registered.

"Yeah. I met you at Jesse Turner's trial a couple years back."

Her eyes widened. "I remember. You replaced the old Sheriff, the one I gave my initial statement to."

"That's right."

Her shoulders slumped. "Jesse's dead. Walker killed him. Oh, God, it was terrible. He was so violent."

"We found Jesse's body," Savage said softly.

She let out a loud sob. "I knew it. I knew he couldn't survive that."

"He was alive when we found him," Thorpe cut in. She turned to look at the deputy, a slim, weedy guy, drenched to the bone. His clothes were filthy, there were leaves in his hair, and his glasses were misted up.

"He was?"

"He told us in which direction Walker took you. We couldn't have found you without his help."

Jesse had saved her life. He'd sent these officers after her.

Unable to help it, she started crying. "I'm sorry." Sniffing, she pressed her fists into her eyes as if to stop the tears.

"Where is this Walker now?" the Sheriff asked.

"We stopped in the outcrop." She shuddered and tried to pull herself together. "I hit him with a stick. He'll come after me, though. It won't be long."

"We have backup coming soon," the deputy told her.

"How soon?" These two might have been law enforcement, but it was still just the two of them against a violent monster, and they looked bedraggled, like they'd been out here a while.

"He's got a gun," she warned them. "It was Jesse's."

The Sheriff nodded like he already knew that. "Thorpe, you take Candy back to the clearing and wait for the chopper."

"You can't go after Dixon on your own," Thorpe insisted. "It's too dangerous."

"Dixon?" She glanced at the sheriff.

"It's his real name," he told her. "Ernest Dixon."

Candy snorted. "He told me his name was Walker, but I'm not surprised that was a lie." Everything else was.

"Where is the outcrop?" the Sheriff asked.

She explained as best she could, but she'd taken such a haphazard route to get here that she couldn't be sure.

"I'll find it," he said. "I remember that outcrop. We walked straight past it when we first smelled the smoke. The rain must have thrown us off the trail."

"I don't think you should go alone," his deputy said, pushing his glasses up his nose. "This guy's dangerous."

"He's right," she whimpered, even though she didn't want to be left alone.

Savage studied her. "You need medical attention. Your feet are cut to shreds."

They were hurting now that she'd stopped running. Cuts and grazes covered her lower legs and ankles, but that was nothing compared to the mess underneath.

"I'll be okay," she gritted out, but then wobbled. It was the deputy, Thorpe, who put his arm out to steady her.

"I'll help you." He was so sweet. "Lean on me, it'll take some of the pressure off."

Savage nodded, then turned away to go after Walker. Together, they hobbled into the clearing to await the helicopter.

SAVAGE WATCHED THEM GO, then drew his gun and checked it to make sure he had one in the chamber. He wasn't playing games here. Dixon, or Walker—or whatever the hell his name was—was going down. Walker had killed two men that Savage knew of, and he'd kidnapped Candy. There were probably others, along with that young girl in New Mexico. The serial killer's bloody rampage was about to come to an abrupt halt.

He progressed cautiously, careful to not make a sound. His thigh was burning, but he didn't stop to check it. There would be plenty of time for that later when Walker was in custody. He gritted his teeth against the pain and kept going.

The outcrop loomed ahead, gaping like an open mouth on the side of the mountain. Going closer, he saw the smoke.

The rain was letting up now, improving visibility. Hiding behind a tree, Savage surveyed the makeshift camp. There was Candy's backpack, lying against the wall. A small fire glowed at the entrance, protected from the rain. It wasn't a deep cave, more of a shallow recess. A dark blue backpack was just visible from behind a rock. He moved closer. Was Walker there too?

Crouching behind a thick tree with leafy branches, he tried to get a better look. The campsite appeared to be empty. Walker wasn't there.

He was about to sneak forward when a branch cracked behind him. Swinging around, he saw Walker holding a log like a tennis racquet. Before he could duck, Walker swung, striking Savage on the side of the head—and his world went dark.

NINETEEN

CANDY CLUNG to Thorpe as they made their way back to the clearing. It was still raining, more of a drizzle now.

"The helicopter will be here soon," the deputy said.

She hoped he was right. It wouldn't take Walker long to come after her.

"Is the Sheriff really going after Walker by himself?" she asked.

"Yeah." The deputy wanted to be with him, she could tell.

"You can leave me in the clearing," she offered, as he helped her over a fallen log. "If you want to go back and help him." They had no idea what kind of monster they were dealing with.

Thorpe hesitated, torn. "It's okay, I should stay with you."

A wave of weariness hit her, and her legs gave out. Only Thorpe's arm around her waist prevented her from collapsing onto the wet ground. "You okay?"

She gave a weak nod. "Yeah, although I could kill a burger right now."

"Haven't had much to eat, eh?"

"Nothing for a few days." Her stomach rumbled at the talk of food.

Her mouth was parched, too. "He barely gave me any water. I don't think he was going to keep me alive for very long."

"Did he say what he was planning to do with you?" Thorpe asked.

"Only that he had something special in mind." She shivered. "He's crazy. I think he's done this before. Killed women, I mean."

Thorpe frowned. "What makes you say that?"

"It was the way he said it, like he relished the opportunity."

Thorpe helped her across a gurgling stream. She was grateful for his physical support. Without it, she didn't think she'd get very far. The drizzle seemed lighter now. "Don't think about it anymore. You're safe now."

Safe. That was something she hadn't felt since this whole thing started. Ironic, since the sole reason she'd left Hawk's Landing was, so she'd be safe.

"Then there's the cabin," she said, thinking about where Walker had been going to take her.

The deputy jerked his head towards her. "What cabin?"

"That's where we were headed, to a cabin in the forest. I don't know where exactly, only that it was close. He was trying to get there by nightfall, but then it started raining."

"Did it belong to him?"

She shook her head. "I think it belonged to one of his victims." She swallowed against her dry throat. "He said it was someone he knew."

Thorpe pursed his lips. "We'll have to look into that."

She knew what he was thinking. That Walker could have taken other victims there. Victims they didn't know about.

"Is he a serial killer?" she whispered.

Thorpe met her gaze, his voice low. "It's looking like it."

Candy drew in a sharp breath. She'd been in the clutches of a raging psychopath. What the hell? All because Zeb had told her to get out of town.

Coming up here had seemed like such a good idea at the time. It was quiet, peaceful, no one around to bother her. Her happy place. The hiking trail was too tough for beginners, which meant the man looking for her would never attempt it.

How could she have known it would turn out like this? She stifled a laugh. Talk about ironic. All she'd done was replace one dangerous man with another—a serial killer.

She was lucky to be alive.

"Thank you," she murmured, gratitude washing over her. "Thank you for coming for me."

Thorpe smiled. "It's what we do, ma'am. I'm just glad you're alive."

"What now?" She asked when they reached the small clearing. It was hard to believe a helicopter could land here. The pilot must be very skilled. On edge, she strained her ears but couldn't hear anything in the way of rotor blades.

"We wait." Thorpe lowered her down on a boulder. It was dripping wet but had a flat enough surface to make a decent chair. She sank down, glad to get the weight off her feet.

"Here, drink some water." Gratefully, she took his flask and lifted it to her lips. "I think I have a protein bar somewhere."

She watched as he rummaged through his backpack, finally pulling out a flattened energy bar. "Sorry, it's a little squashed."

"I don't care." To her, it was the most wonderful thing on the planet. She ripped the wrapper off and devoured it.

"Thank you," she mumbled, her mouth full.

He grinned. "Can't have you passing out on me." He took out the first aid kit. "Let me look at your feet. I might be able to make you a little more comfortable."

Feeling shy, she let him inspect her shredded soles.

He cringed. "That looks painful. I'll disinfect the cuts and wrap some gauze around them, but you'll need to get to a doctor. The deeper ones might need stitches."

She nodded, then sucked in a breath as the antiseptic spray hit her feet.

"What happened to your shoes?" he asked as he applied the gauze.

"Walker made me take them off." She stuffed the last of the energy bar into her mouth. "To make it harder for me to run away."

Thorpe grunted.

"I grew up in these parts," she continued. She felt comfortable with the deputy now. He had been so sweet. "I've been hiking the Stony Ridge trail since I was a teenager."

He glanced up at her. Kind eyes, she thought. Soft and pale blue, with a determined edge to them. She liked that.

"Lucky for you," he said, then cleared his throat. "That you got away anyway, I mean." He fell over his words. Was he flustered?

"Lucky me." Candy became conscious of her disheveled state. Her hair must be a mass of frizzy tangles, and her clothes were torn and covered in mud. Self-conscious, she ran a hand through the tangles, but it got stuck right away. Sighing, she dropped her arm. What was the point?

Still, the look in the young deputy's gaze made her feel warm and tingly. He finished wrapping her feet with gauze. A soft touch, gentle hands.

"That'll do for now." He packed up the kit and placed the box back into his backpack. "Hopefully it'll give you some relief."

"Thank you." She cleared her throat. "I'm sorry, I don't know your first name?"

"Kevin." His cheeks colored. "Kevin Thorpe."

"Thank you, Kevin."

"You're welcome."

They stared at each other for a short moment, when she saw a shadow behind Thorpe and looked up.

She screamed. It couldn't be.

Thorpe spun around, going for his gun. He was too slow. Walker pulled the trigger. It was so loud it made her ears ring.

At such a close distance, he couldn't miss. Thorpe took the shot in the torso and flew backwards, landing several feet away. He didn't move.

Candy leaped up to go to him, but Walker grabbed her wrist,

twisting it painfully. "No, you don't," he growled. "You're coming with me."

"No!" she sobbed, but he dragged her away, leaving Thorpe's unmoving body next to the boulder.

TWENTY

SAVAGE WOKE in a world of pain.

What the—?

His head felt like a herd of buffalo was marching through it. His vision was blurry when he opened his eyes. Groaning, he tried to sit up, but found he couldn't move. His hands were bound behind his back, and a thick rope bound his ankles. He wasn't going anywhere.

The contents of his backpack were spread out on the ground. Gloves, evidence bags, transponder flags to mark the scene of the crime.

Slowly, it came back. Creeping towards the recess, the fire, the backpacks, then the branch breaking behind him and *wham*—the blow to the head.

Walker.

The tender spot on his head made him wince. He wondered how long he'd been out. An hour? A day? Was he concussed? That would explain the blurred vision.

He shifted after hearing a muted sob. His heart dropped.

No.

"Candy?" He murmured.

The young woman was bound and gagged and propped up against

the back of the shallow cave. Tears streamed down her face, making it hard to breathe. She sniveled. Walker pulled the gag out of her mouth. "One word and I'll cut your tongue out." She gave a terrified nod.

It was then Savage realized she was wearing his handcuffs.

There was no sign of Thorpe.

Savage's heart rate escalated. "Where's my deputy?" he rasped.

Walker glanced over. He'd been inspecting Savage's Glock. "Welcome back."

"What have you done with him?"

"Nothing, he's back at the clearing."

"He's dead!" Candy blurted. "*He* shot him at point blank range." She glared at Walker, who marched over and stuffed the filthy gag back into her mouth.

"You don't learn, do you? Stupid bitch!"

Candy's eyes blazed into his.

Thorpe, dead?

Savage's brain struggled to process the news. No, he couldn't be. Not Thorpe. His deputy had been such an asset. A fast learner, filled with determination. A smart detective. A friend. Savage couldn't believe he was dead.

"What happened?" he whispered.

"Like she said." Walker marched up and crouched down in front of him. Close, but not close enough. Not that Savage could do anything anyway, with his hands and feet bound. He wriggled, frustrated. Walker laughed. "Relax, Sheriff. You're not going anywhere."

"Why am I still here?" Savage asked, taking stock of his surroundings. Jesse's revolver lay on a flat rock by the fire. "Why didn't you kill me?"

A nonchalant shrug. "I thought maybe we could have a chat."

"A chat? We've got nothing to talk about."

"Think of it as a role reversal. I'm in charge now. You're the prisoner. We're going to have ourselves a little interrogation." He laughed, a hollow, creepy sound. Savage supposed Walker was what you might call handsome. Even features, thick hair, a strong physique. Except with his lips curled back in a snarl, his forehead pinched, and that manic glint in his eyes, he looked plain evil. The guy was crazy. No doubt about it.

"Of course, if you don't want to, we can always skip that part. Go straight to the next step."

Savage frowned. "Which is?"

Walker raised the handgun. "Shooting you in the goddamn head." Glaring at Savage, he shoved the weapon into the back of his shorts. Savage noticed the grimace as Walker put his hand behind his back.

"Jesse said he got a shot off." He nodded to Walker's shoulder. "Pity it was wide. A few inches to the left and it would have hit the bullseye."

Walker's face reddened. "What are you talking about?"

"Oh, you thought you'd killed him when you brained him with that rock? Nah, he survived, at least long enough to tell us who attacked him." Savage's gaze hardened. "You're going down, Walker. It's just a matter of time."

Walker raised an eyebrow. "I'm surprised he lived long enough to say anything."

Candy suppressed a sob.

The killer picked up the revolver and pointed it at Savage's face.

How many bullets were in the gun? Five? Four? Less? Savage gave a stiff nod. "Fine."

A chuckle. "Makes a change, don't it?"

Candy gaped at the two of them, her eyes huge. If she could speak, she'd probably be asking what the hell he was doing. Why was he indulging this asshole? The answer was, he was stalling for time. The chopper was on its way. He had to hang on for as long as possible, keep the psycho talking until help arrived. Then hope to hell Walker didn't shoot them both. This was the only play they had.

"So." Walker sat down in front of Savage, gritting his teeth as the jolt reverberated to his shoulder. "How does it feel being on the other side of the table?"

Savage managed a small shrug. "No different. Talking is talking."

The gun pointed at his head remained steady. "Except this time, I'm asking the questions."

They locked eyes. Walker, smug and arrogant despite his wound and situation. Savage, defiant and hostile. "So ask."

That took some of the wind out of Walker's sails. "Do you even know how many lives you've ruined?"

"Excuse me?"

"How many people have you put away?"

"Criminals, you mean?" Savage pretended to think. "I've put away plenty of criminals, and they all deserved it."

"I don't believe you," Walker said. The firelight turned his expression diabolical. A wild joker smile with dirty cheeks and hooded eyes.

"I can't help that."

"How many of those people got a chance to tell their side of the story?"

"All of them, I hope." Savage studied Walker. "They go to trial before prison, you know? It's called a democracy. Although, that bit doesn't have anything to do with me"

A grunt.

"You referring to your last run-in with the law?" Savage guessed.

Walker's eyes narrowed. "How'd you know about that?"

"I've read your file, Ernest Dixon. I know exactly who you are—and what you've done. That twenty-one-year-old from New Mexico?" He arched an eyebrow.

Walker hesitated, then smiled. "Ah, Mia." The faraway look in Walker's eyes was chilling. Savage waited, giving Walker space to talk.

"She was special. Took a long time to die."

Candy cringed and strained against her ties.

"I held her hand while she ebbed away. Stroked her face. We had fun, me and her."

The man was sick. Savage didn't want to think about what he'd done to Mia before she'd died. "Did you hit her over the head with a rock, too?"

"It's the best way. You can see the life draining out of them. The confusion, the fear." He looked almost euphoric.

Candy squeezed her eyes shut and turned away. Savage held his gaze. "Like Mark Stillwell? Jesse Turner?"

Walker blinked and turned his attention back to Savage. "Just like them, yeah. But what about you, Sheriff? Have you ever killed a man?"

Savage didn't reply.

"Of *course* you have. How'd it make you feel?"

Savage gazed through Walker into the past. He was back in Denver, responding to the Code 10 call with his field training officer, Clinton Briggs.

Gunfire. Screams. People streaming out of the building in blood-soaked clothes.

He and Briggs were the first on the scene.

The shooter, a disgruntled former employee, was somewhere in the building. Shots had been heard, followed by terrified screams. A witness had seen him walk in holding a shotgun and called the police. Savage and Briggs split up to search for him.

Savage remembered walking down the corridor, his government-issued Glock 22 pressed out in front of him, terrified as to what he might encounter. It was his first real Code 10.

An open office door. Moans from the victims. Blood seeping out into the corridor.

Heart hammering, he radioed Briggs. "He's on my side." The response had been mere static. Had his field training officer even heard the call?

A loud click as a magazine was seated, followed by the bolt release. The gunman was only feet away.

Fate picked us today. That's what Briggs had said before they'd gone into the building, then he'd smiled. *Let's not let her down.*

Mouth dry, palms sweaty, Savage approached the door. Months of training drills at the academy flashed through his head, but nothing had prepared him for this. The fear was unlike anything he'd ever known. The knowledge that he could take another human life clawed at his conscience. He hadn't yet developed the steely eyed determination that came with saving lives.

He was about to enter when the shooter stepped out into the hallway. His weapon was still aimed at the man on the floor. He'd had to reload to finish the victim off.

"Please," begged the wounded man. "Please don't—"

Spotting Savage in his peripheral vision, the shooter spun around, his attention diverted. That split second was all it took. Savage pulled the trigger and felt the gun kick. Four times. Center mass. The guy didn't stand a chance.

Later, Savage found out the man on the office floor had lived. By killing the shooter, he'd saved the man's life. He'd answered Fate's call.

"I said, how'd it make you feel?" Walker kicked at Savage's bound feet.

"Like shit," he snapped. He'd battled to deal with the guilt, to put it into perspective. Eventually, he'd succeeded. An act of violence to end more acts of violence. That was what it boiled down to. And he'd done it again, several times during his ten-year career in Denver Homicide. That was the job. He received no pleasure from it. Not like this psycho here.

Walker shook his head. "There's nothing like it. You must have felt it, the power over another human being."

Savage said nothing.

"You know, you and me, we're not that different."

What the hell was he talking about?

"In fact, I'll bet you've killed more men than I have."

Savage glared at him. As much as he hated to admit it, Walker did have a point.

"Tell me, what do you tell yourself when you go to sleep at night? How do you justify those kills?"

When Savage didn't answer, Walker laughed. "When you wake up in the morning and you look in the mirror, do you have to convince yourself you're not the bad guy?"

"Shut up."

Ignoring him, Walker picked up Savage's cellphone and glanced at the screen. "I've got an idea."

Gritting his teeth, Savage thought about how much he'd like to bury his fist in Walker's smirking face right about now.

"Look up." He held the device up to Savage's face. He turned his head, but it was too late. The screen flashed on.

Damnit.

Now Walker had access to Savage's phone, his apps, his contacts. Still, reception was sketchy. Walker wouldn't be able to do much out here.

Walker turned the camera on. "Any final words?"

Scowling, Savage refused to look up.

Annoyed, Walker stomped his foot onto Savage's leg, where the bear had clawed him. He growled as pain radiated through his body.

"You sure you have nothing to say?"

Savage opened his eyes and glared at his tormentor. "It'll be fun ripping your head off, Walker."

To his surprise, Walker roared with laughter. Pocketing the phone, he took out a blade.

This is it. Savage watched the blade inch closer. *It's over.*

TWENTY-ONE

BECKY SINCLAIR HELD the wheel in one hand and her phone in the other. "What do you mean, they don't have one?" she yelled, as she slowed down to take a corner. "They're the State Police."

"Their helicopter is down for maintenance," Barbara told her.

Of all the fucking times.

"They can't only have one." Sinclair opened up now that she was on the straight. She hadn't heard from Thorpe or Savage since that last short call hours ago. They'd be waiting for a chopper and she couldn't get one to them. What a disaster.

Despite several calls, neither Thorpe nor Savage picked up. Straight to voicemail. They were out of range again, or their phones had been switched off or destroyed. Regardless, there was no way to contact them about the delay.

"The nearest helicopter is in Denver," Barbara replied. "It'd take too long for them to get it down this far south."

Crap. Now what?

"What do you want me to do?" Barbara's voice was weak. They were all worried about the team in the mountains.

"I don't know." Sinclair approached an unmarked turnoff and veered hard left, causing the tires to screech and spin as they left the paved road.

"Where are you?" Barbara asked. With Littleton in the hospital, the small sheriff's department was empty except for her and Barbara.

"I'VE GOT AN IDEA," Sinclair said, roaring up the winding track, kicking up a cloud of red dirt behind her. "I'll call you back." She hung up. Tall trees masked the secluded property at the end, and it was only when she rounded a bend that the angled rise of the wood-shingled roof came into view.

It had been a while since she'd been here, back when Hatch had been working as a de facto member of their department.

Hatch.

She'd learned so much from the confident military veteran. Having Hatch as part of the team had shown Sinclair the type of cop she wanted to be. Dedicated. Fearless. Honorable.

Yes, she mused. They'd all learned a great deal from Hatch.

This was her mother's property. Jasmine Hatch. Known for her spirit, enduring beauty, and, of course, her coffee. Jasmine made the best brew in the county, bar none. But it wasn't the coffee she was here for today. Sinclair needed to speak to Jed, Jasmine's partner.

Jedediah Russell.

Another veteran and ex-member of the 101st Airborne Division. The door opened, and the man appeared on the doorstep as her car roared up the drive.

"Evening, Jed," Sinclair said, getting out of the vehicle.

"Evening."

He surveyed her pinched expression as she marched up to the porch. "What's up?"

Sinclair didn't bother to deny it. "We've got a situation. I'm all out of ideas and I need your help."

"You'd better come in." The old timer led her into the kitchen where she smelled roasted coffee beans. Jasmine was clearing up after their evening meal and shot a smile in Sinclair's direction. "Good to see you again, Becky."

"You too, Jasmine. I'm sorry to barge in like this."

Jasmine shook her head. "No need to apologize. Is Savage all right?"

"I don't know." Sighing, she sat in the chair Jed had pulled out for her. Jasmine poured them all a cup and took a seat. "He's not answering his phone."

"What can we do to help?" Jed cut to the chase.

Sinclair looked at him. "Jed, can you fly a helicopter?"

"Oh, boy," whispered Jasmine.

"Sure, back in the day." He didn't say he couldn't fly one now.

"Savage and Thorpe are pursuing a serial killer up behind Stony Ridge. They need backup. Now. I haven't been able to find a single chopper to get airborne anytime soon."

Jed shrugged. "Unless you have a chopper I can fly, I'm useless."

"I didn't say I couldn't get one," she explained.

"Okay." Jed glanced at Jasmine. "So where is this chopper I'm going to fly?"

"That's just it." Sinclair wrapped her hands around the mug. "We're going to steal one."

———

SAVAGE STEELED himself as Walker leaned down with the blade. Instead of burying it in his torso or stomach or kidneys, as he'd expected, Walker cut through the rope that bound Savage's ankles.

"Hold me up, and I'll kill you."

It took a moment for the words to sink in. Walker wasn't going to attack him. Instead, he wanted the Sheriff to get up and walk. Savage breathed a silent sigh of relief. They were on the move. Walker knew help was coming and wanted to get away from this spot as soon as possible. Smart move.

"Where are we going?" Savage rolled onto his stomach to get to his feet. Something dug into his hip. Glancing down, he saw one of the little transponder flags. Shifting back onto his back, he cupped it in his hand. Then, using the cave wall as leverage, he stood up.

With his hands hidden, he snapped the flag off the transponder and dropped it into his back pocket.

Candy stood more easily, but her haunted eyes stared at Savage. Walker had freaked her out. He shot her a reassuring smile, or at least what he hoped was a smile. It was more of a grimace.

The transponder would relay their position. Eventually, someone would find them.

She looked away, hopeless.

They set off, Candy still in cuffs, Savage with his hands tied behind his back. Walker had both the revolver and service pistol, although it was the Glock that was pointed at Savage's back as he limped along.

Candy had a long rope looped around her waist. Walker had tied the other end to his wrist so that his hand was free to carry the flashlight. The ground was dark, the trees obscuring the faint light of the moon.

"She'll run the first chance she gets," he explained when he caught Savage studying the rope. "If you try anything, I'll just shoot you in the back."

Savage didn't want to put that to the test. They walked on for half a mile. He was conscious that every step took them further from the clearing. Even with the transponder active, the only place the chopper could land was in that clearing.

It was getting dark, the sun having set an hour ago. Becca would be worried. She'd call the station only to have Barbara confirm they hadn't heard from him in hours.

Where the hell was that chopper?

Savage's leg seized up and he stumbled to the ground. Walker kicked him in the ribs. "Get up."

Savage took his time getting up. Every second counted. Candy was panting. Malnourished and dehydrated, she wouldn't last long. Even Walker was showing the strain. His arm hung uselessly by his side, his hand red with dried blood. The Glock in his other hand remained stable.

"Go down again and you'll stay there," Walker warned.

Savage could hear Walker's ragged breathing behind him. It was the one thing that kept him going. The thought that their captor was suffering as much, if not more, than they were.

As darkness set in, they headed into a canyon. The elevation changed, and the ground became steep and uneven. Trees twisted around them, casting crooked shadows, and it was difficult to see more than a few feet ahead. There was no sign of the crescent moon. It seemed to have deserted them, too.

With every step, the pain in Savage's leg got worse, and his spirits sank. They had to stop. Had to get back to the clearing. How far had they walked now? A mile? Two?

A short while later, they heard a rushing sound and came to a fast-flowing creek. Candy collapsed, her legs giving out on the bank.

Savage knelt beside her. "Candy? Candy, can you hear me?"

Walker jerked the rope like he was whipping a horse.

"Stop it!" Savage shouted. "Can't you see she needs a break? Do you have any water?"

Walker stared down at her as if he was deciding whether to shoot her or not.

"Water?" Savage repeated, distracting him.

Candy's head dropped forward.

"Stay down for as long as you can," Savage murmured in her ear. "Help is coming, but we've got to get back to the clearing."

She gave a tiny moan. He wasn't sure if she'd registered what he'd said.

Reluctantly, Walker got the canister out of his backpack and held it up to Candy's lips. Her eyes fluttered open, and she took a sip, water dribbling down her chin.

"That's enough." Walker retook control of the situation. "Get up, both of you."

"I can't," she whimpered. Savage wasn't sure if she was playing along or really meant it. Her eyes were sunken into her pale face, and she could barely hold her head up, let alone walk. Savage frowned, worried. With his leg, he doubted he'd be able to carry her back up the hill. Rescue seemed to be more and more unlikely.

Walker gritted his teeth. "Get up, or I'll kill you both."

Candy staggered to her feet, then bent down to help Savage, whose hands were still tied behind his back. With some difficulty, Savage got to his feet, but no sooner was he upright when their captor put a foot on his back and kicked him over. "Stay away from her."

Savage hit the rocky ground beside the creek, landing on his shoulder. Pain radiated up his arm.

"What's this?" Walker stood where Savage had been kneeling.

No. No. No.

The transponder. It had fallen out of his pocket when Walker had kicked him.

Their captor inspected the flashing device. "They're *tracking* us?" Fury contorted his features, and he dropped the transponder and crushed it underfoot.

When he looked up, his gaze held pure hatred. "You're dead, Savage."

TWENTY-TWO

SINCLAIR and Jed crept along the tarmac toward the hangar.

"Are you sure about this?" Jed asked, as they flattened themselves against the wall. It was a still night, no wind and only a sliver of moon. Perfect for flying.

"Yes. We have no other option."

She'd seen the crop helicopters refuel the previous day when she'd driven past.

"We could just ask them."

Sinclair shot him a look. "You know as well as I do that it'll take days to get the paperwork. Savage is in trouble. He needs us now."

Jed gave a sharp nod. "Okay then. Let's do this." He raised the hangar door, hearing it groan as it went up.

Sinclair looked around. "We'll have to be quick. They'll have heard that."

She was right.

A shout rang out from across the tarmac and two men began walking toward them. They weren't armed—at least she didn't think they were—except with flashlights. The beams bounced off the ground as they moved.

"Quick" Sinclair said.

Jed climbed into the neat red and white Bell 206. The spray booms were still attached, but that couldn't be helped. There was no time to remove them.

Sinclair hopped in beside him and buckled up. "Let's go."

Jed stared at the controls.

"You do know how to fly this thing, right?" She asked, her heart skipping a beat.

"Give me a second. It's been a while." His eyes roamed over the controls, then he began pressing buttons. The rotors started to spin.

The men, still five hundred yards away at the small airfield tower, broke into a run. The rotors spun faster, filling the hangar with a high-pitched scream. It got louder and louder until it was deafening.

"Ear guards on," Jed yelled, handing her a pair.

She pulled them over her ears, muffling the sound. The helicopter began to shake. She glanced at Jed, whose eyes were locked on the controls.

One of the men shouted at them to stop.

Too late, Sinclair thought, as the machine rose off the ground. It hovered for a moment, then thudded back down onto the skids.

Sinclair sent him a worried look.

"I'm getting there," Jed muttered, toggling the stick. They were still in the building, the hangar roof above them.

"Come on," murmured Sinclair, as the men reached the hangar.

The helicopter rose again, then surged out of the hangar, forcing the two men to jump out of the way.

Yes!

They cleared the roof with what felt like inches to spare.

"Great job!" Sinclair shouted. She looked down at the men. One spoke urgently into his walkie-talkie, the other shouted, gesturing at the rising helicopter.

She resisted the urge to wave.

They gained altitude, putting distance between them and the scene of their transgression. Jed was enjoying himself now. "Hell, I didn't think I'd ever fly again."

She smiled at the exuberant look on his face. A faded military tattoo was just visible on his right forearm underneath his folded shirt sleeve. Screaming Eagles, she remembered Hatch telling her. The 101st Airborne Division. "How long has it been?"

"Too long. Last time I flew was early '72. We were the last division to leave Vietnam. That was one hell of a mission."

"What happened?" she asked. They had some time to kill as they headed over the town.

"We crashed."

"What?" Her eyes widened.

"We were flying into Laos to cut off enemy supply lines when we got shot down. Crashed in the jungle. Took us two weeks to find our way out."

Sinclair stared at him. "Were you hurt?"

"Not me. The pilot was, though. He died before we could evacuate. The rest of us managed to hike back to base."

She could see by the look in his eyes that he hadn't forgotten. "I'm sorry."

He shrugged. "It was a long time ago."

"You haven't flown since?"

Jed shook his head. "Nah. We were transported back to Fort Campbell soon after that. Our part in the war was over. I left the army after that."

Sinclair nodded. Hawk's Landing twinkled in the twilight below them. "What's our ETA?" she asked, as the jagged peaks loomed in front of them.

"Twenty minutes."

"I have their last coordinates here." She checked her phone. "Thorpe said there was a small clearing."

"We'll need one to land," Jed confirmed. "Especially with these spray booms on the bottom."

The Bell 206 rose like a hawk in the air, scaling the peaks with ease. "That's Stony Ridge, down there." He nodded outside the window.

Sinclair looked down at the rocky ledge. It was too dark to make out the trail, but the jagged peak looked menacing in the near darkness.

Jed flew over the aspen forest, his eyes flickering over the levers and gauges, making sure everything was as it should be. "That it?"

Sinclair squinted down but couldn't see anything other than trees. A dark green field of broccoli. "I don't see a clearing."

"Looks like we're right over it."

She checked the coordinates. "Reads that way."

"It's going to be tight."

She swallowed. "Will we make it?"

"Let's find out." He lowered the helicopter to just above tree level, the lights underneath illuminated the foliage. The broccoli heads rocked from side to side, buffeted by the downdraft. "My flight instructor once told me something I'll never forget."

She raised an eyebrow. "What's that?"

"Take-off is optional. Landing is mandatory." She forced a laugh.

Slowly, Jed maneuvered the helicopter down into the clearing. Dust swirled around them. The tree branches heaved back and forth in a crazy head-banging dance. One tapped the crop boom, and the chopper wobbled.

Jed wrestled with the control, and Sinclair closed her eyes as they rose a couple of feet into the air.

"It's gonna be tight," Jed muttered, lining them up again.

Sinclair was almost afraid to look down at the clearing. It was a swirling mass of dust and debris. An apocalyptic black hole. She couldn't see where the trees ended, and the clearing began, let alone fit the chopper through it.

Jed worked the throttle, battling to keep the helicopter stable as they sank into the dust storm. The rotors clipped the trees around them, sending leaves and bits of branches flying.

Please let us make it, Sinclair prayed.

She wondered where Savage and Thorpe were, and whether they'd managed to rescue Candy. They had to get on the ground.

"It's too close." Jed gave up and lifted the machine back above the tree line.

Crap.

"Are you sure?" She ran a hand through her hair. Where else could they land? There didn't appear to be anywhere suitable for miles.

"One more time," he gritted, steely determination written all over his face.

Sinclair found she was crossing her fingers.

"Come on, Jed. You can do it."

TWENTY-THREE

SAVAGE LAY SPRAWLED on the wet ground, waiting for the shot that would end his life—but it never came. Walker seemed at odds with himself, not knowing what to do. In the one hand, he held the gun, sticky with his own blood. In the other, he had the flashlight.

It would be easiest to take the shot, but Walker ended up raising the hand with the flashlight in it. Perhaps he preferred to beat his victims to death.

"I'm going to kill you, Savage," he growled, moving forward.

At least that gave him a fighting chance.

Walker snarled and leaped towards him, holding the flashlight in the air like a hammer. Savage tried to scoot backwards, but there was nowhere to go. Behind him, the creek rushed its way through the canyon. The whitewater had been whipped to a frenzy on account of the rain, and if he moved back any further, he'd go under. It was already lapping at his clothes.

Walker bore down on Savage, jaw clenched, veins bulging in his neck. Rage had contorted his features so that his face resembled a demonic mask. He swung the flashlight down. Savage twisted away in a fruitless attempt to protect his head. Instead of a crushing blow, he heard a high-pitched scream. He looked up just in time to see Candy, barefoot, blond hair flying, bolt out of the shadows and barrel into Walker. The sudden impact threw the killer off balance. He keeled over, dropping the flashlight.

Still on the ground, Savage pivoted and dug his boot heel into Walker's wound. The man screamed, releasing the gun to clutch his shoulder.

Savage kicked the Glock into the whitewater. Thank goodness the revolver was still in Walker's backpack, out of reach. Grunting, Savage got to his feet. Candy had picked herself up off the cold, wet ground and was glaring at Walker like she wanted to kill him. Her hands were clenched into tight fists. Walker rolled around on the creek bank, his face twisted in agony.

Candy took a step toward him.

"No," Savage barked. "Leave him. We have to go."

She looked like she might refuse, but then stepped away, leaving Walker writhing on the riverbank. Together, they took off up the hill in the direction they'd come.

Despite her weakened state, Candy moved faster than he could with his mauled leg and tightly bound wrists. Every step was an effort. The pain was beginning to pulsate down his leg, and he feared it might get infected. He needed a tetanus shot, and soon.

Her hands were cuffed in front of her so she could hold them up to protect her face from swinging branches. He wasn't so lucky, but he kept his face bowed to ward off the worst of it.

As soon as they'd gotten far enough away from Walker, Savage called a halt. They were both panting. "Candy, can you untie me?"

She inspected the knot. "I don't know. I can try."

It took a while, but she wriggled the knot loose and freed his wrists.

"Thank you." He waved his arms around to get more circulation. Unfortunately, Walker had the keys to the handcuffs, so he couldn't do the same for her.

"We'd better keep going," he said, once he could feel his fingers. "Let's head to the clearing."

In the distance, they heard the faint but very welcome whap-whap of rotor blades. Savage broke into a grin. "Hear that? That's for us."

Candy managed a tired smile. "Thank God."

They kept going, stumbling every few feet. It was too dark to make out the hidden roots and bushes in their way, and they didn't have Walker's flashlight. Savage noticed that, despite her ruined feet and exhaustion, Candy didn't complain once. She was tough.

It was slow going, but they persevered. The sound from the helicopter got louder. Almost there.

He glanced up but couldn't see anything through the trees. Judging by the noise level, they had to be beneath it.

A loud bang made them jump.

"He's shooting at us," Candy yelped as a bullet whistled past and buried itself in a nearby fir tree with a dull thud.

"Can't have many bullets left," Savage muttered.

"How close are we to the clearing?" There was fear in her voice.

"Almost there. Keep going."

Several more bullets flew past. Four, three, two... Savage counted them off in his head. With Jesse's shot that caught Walker in the shoulder, that left one.

They reached the clearing. Hovering above it was a small but functional helicopter. It was the most beautiful sight he'd ever seen.

"It's here!" Candy was about to run towards it when Savage called, "Wait."

She stopped. "What? They're about to land. Come on."

"The shooting stopped."

"So?"

"He might have one more shot left." If he let Candy run blindly into the clearing, she could end up taking that last bullet.

She hesitated, glancing around. "What should we do?"

There was a crack in the gloom behind them. Walker was stalking them, closing in.

"Wait here." Savage made a snap decision. "I'll draw him out and when the helicopter lands, run for it." One bullet. Two targets. He couldn't fire at them both.

Candy's voice was a whimper. "What about you?"

"I'll be right behind you. But I need to distract Walker long enough for you to get to the chopper."

There was a soft rustle as she ran towards him and threw her arms around his neck. "Thank you," she whispered. "For everything."

Then she was gone, melting into the shadows.

The rotor downwash kicked up dust and debris. Savage squinted to protect his eyes. The pilot was hovering, looking for a suitable place to land. The clearing was a small one, and those booms on the underside made maneuvering difficult. Savage didn't know much about flying, but he did know that if the pilot hit a tree or a rock, the chopper could spin out of control.

He saw a flash of silver hair behind a large boulder. Candy was hunkering behind a rock, waiting for the skids to touch down so she could run for safety. Straining his eyes, he made out Sinclair's figure in the cockpit, along with the pilot. Lithe, bearded, and bending over the controls.

Was that Jed?

Savage snuck back the way he'd come, keeping low. Walker was easy to spot, as he was using a flashlight. As long as Savage kept the trees between himself and his adversary, he wouldn't be seen.

Walker moved fast, heading towards the helicopter. Even in the murky undercarriage lights of the chopper, Savage could make out the revolver in Walker's hand.

Fate chose me that day.

Savage hid behind a tree stump, out of sight. Walker came closer, an urgency in his step. His victims were getting away. If he wanted to stop them, he had to do it now. He was operating on pure adrenaline and rage. With one last bullet, he had to make it count.

Savage bent down and felt around for something he could use as a weapon. His fingers closed around a thick branch about the size of his wrist.

That would have to do.

Walker strode past.

Now!

Savage jumped out from behind the stump and swung.

TWENTY-FOUR

SAVAGE DESCENDED on Walker like an avenging angel. With a blood-curdling yell, he raised the stick, aiming for the killer's chest. Whether it was his lingering concussion or fatigued state, Savage's aim was off, and Walker was stronger than he looked, even with the bleeding shoulder. The killer dodged the onslaught and the makeshift spear bounced off his left shoulder.

Howling, Walker twisted his body and shoved Savage off balance. His mauled leg collapsed beneath him, but Savage wasn't done yet. Grasping Walker's shirt, he pulled the serial killer over with him and they hit the ground together. Dust burned their eyes from the rotor blades. Leaves whipped up by the force of the wind swirled around them like a twister, twigs and loose pebbles pummeled into their legs and arms.

But Savage felt none of this, his adrenalin was pumping so hard. Walker was his only focus. Scrambling to his knees, Savage lunged for the hand holding the gun, deflecting it in case he got a shot off. One shot was all it would take. But Walker didn't pull the trigger. Not yet. He was saving that last shot for when he was sure he wouldn't miss.

A punch to the gut winded Savage, and he gasped for breath. Another, harder punch, threw him off Walker. He realized too late that

Walker had reverted to his MO and was clutching a sharp-edged rock in his right hand.

Gripping the arm holding the revolver, Savage ignored the blows raining down on his back, and pulled on Walker's arm to smash the gun-hand into the ground.

Stillwell. Jesse. Thorpe. Candy.

Walker yelled in pain, which only served to spur Savage on. It was working. Gritting his teeth, Savage bashed the gun-hand one last time, and the weapon flew out of reach.

Another blow from the rock, the sharp edge penetrating Savage's skin, burning where it had torn through muscle. The pain and exertion had used up what remaining energy he had, and he swayed, dazed.

Sensing Savage's weakness, Walker scrambled to his knees. Rearing up, he brought the rock down again, this time hitting Savage on the head, just missing his temple.

Pain exploded and stars sparkled at the corners of his vision. He groaned and fought not to pass out. Through a blurry haze, Savage spotted the discarded revolver. That was his only chance. He crawled towards it, arm outstretched, but Walker clocked his plan, and stomped on his reaching hand.

He felt the tiny bones snap and howled in agony. The killer's hiking boot came down again, and again, until his hand was a mangled mess on the ground. The chopper had finally set down, and a final blast of dust rendered him blind. He squeezed his eyes shut against the pain and the dust and the knowledge that he'd failed. Walker had the upper hand. Not only that, he had the revolver. He had the final fatal shot.

"You'll never find them all," the killer smirked.

Not now, he wouldn't.

Savage's only hope was that he'd distracted the monster long enough for Candy to get to the chopper. One life out of God-only-knew how many.

Fate chose me today.

He felt a pang as he realized he wouldn't see Becca again. Wouldn't be there for the birth of his child. Wouldn't watch him grow.

Was it worth it? Was everything he'd sacrificed worth it to bring a serial killer down? To save a life? What would Becca say?

He saw her smile, the way her eyes lit up when she looked at him. She'd understand that he'd had no choice. She always understood.

Walker gave a surprised shout and Savage opened his eyes. The muscular man holding the gun was moving from side to side, as if trying to throw something, or someone, off his back. Then he saw the wild blond hair, and the pale arms and legs wrapped around Walker.

Candy!

She'd leaped onto his back and screamed like a banshee, her handcuffs around his neck, choking the life out of him. This time, there was no stopping her.

Walker buckled and fell to his knees. Candy pulled harder, the steel cuffs biting into her slender wrists. Fury gave her strength, and the louder she screamed, the tighter she pulled until Walker's eyes began rolling back.

Savage struggled to his feet, but his legs wouldn't work, and he had no strength in his mashed-up hand. His vision kept moving in and out of focus. He crawled toward the writhing Walker and, with his good hand, wrestled the revolver away from him. It wasn't hard. The man's strength was ebbing. A horrific gurgling noise made his skin crawl. Walker was dying.

"It's okay, Candy," he yelled. "I've got him."

But Candy was too far gone to hear him. A ferocious forest nymph, attacking the jungle predator, squeezing the life out of him.

Savage checked the revolver, opening the chamber. The gun was empty. There were no more bullets left. There never had been.

No last shot.

Just then, Walker keeled over, falling face first onto the hard ground. Unconscious or dead, Savage didn't know. Candy still pulled against him, twisting her wrists, her face contorted with the effort. The screams turned to loud moans. Her slender body trembled with pent-up aggression, hurt, fear, anger. Everything Walker had put her through during the terrible ordeal was pouring out, untapped.

Savage collapsed, spent.

The sound of boots running. Sinclair's arms pulled Candy off Walker. Hysterical sobs as Candy collapsed against the female deputy.

Savage crawled over to Walker and felt for a pulse. None.

The monster was dead.

TWENTY-FIVE

SAVAGE TRIED to push himself off the ground but couldn't. The world spun and he collapsed back down again.

"Sheriff, you okay?" It was Sinclair. She'd come back for him.

He took one last look at Walker's body and nodded. "I will be." His wounds would heal. Candy's, on the other hand, he wasn't so sure about. She'd been through hell in the last couple of days. And now she'd killed a man.

Bending down, Sinclair helped him to his feet.

"Thorpe," he rasped, clutching her arm. "We have to find Thorpe's body."

"What?" Her face paled. "Thorpe's dead?"

"Walker killed him." He spat out the name. "Left his body here in the clearing."

"I didn't know." Her eyes filled with tears, but she blinked them away. Now wasn't the time. They had to get everyone to the chopper and get out of here. There would be time to grieve later.

Sinclair led him to the helicopter. He leaned his weight on her, dragging his mauled leg behind him. His crushed hand hung limply by his side, too painful to move. Yet all he could think about was Thorpe. "We can't leave without him."

"We won't." She helped him into the chopper and Jed turned around to buckle Savage in.

"Jed, I thought that was you. Didn't know you could still fly one of these things."

"Neither did I," he chuckled. "You okay?"

"I will be."

Jed nodded and went back to his pre-flight checks. The rotor blades were spinning again, screaming as they gathered speed. It was hard to see outside the cockpit.

Sinclair jumped back down. "We'll send the troopers up here to get Walker's body," she yelled over the engines. "But I need to find Thorpe."

Just then, Candy yelped and put her hand on the back window. They all turned around.

Out of the dust, like a ghostly apparition, Thorpe walked toward the helicopter. Savage blinked his grainy eyes. Was he hallucinating?

No, it really was his deputy.

Sinclair ran to Thorpe and gave him a hug. Her hair whipped around her face in the downdraft. Then she took his hand and led him to the helicopter.

"We thought you were dead," Savage said, as his colleague climbed in. Despite his aches and pains, he couldn't help grinning.

"Nah, takes more than a couple bullets to put me down." He opened his shirt and exposed a pock-marked ballistic raid vest.

"Thank God." Savage thumped him on the shoulder with his good hand.

Candy leaned over and gave him a warm hug. "I'm so glad you're alive," she said, her face awash with fresh tears.

"You made it," Thorpe said fondly.

She smiled. "Takes more than a crazy psychopath to put me down."

Savage could sense the sparks flying between them. He knew then that Candy was going to be just fine.

"Let's get this bird in the air," he shouted to Jed, who gave a curt nod.

"Yes, sir."

The chopper wobbled as the skids left the ground. Then it rose like a kite, straight up, the spray booms narrowly missing the tops of the trees.

"Great job," Savage said, as Jed turned the helicopter around and flew over the aspen forest.

"You've still got it." Sinclair smiled at the old timer.

He grunted in response.

"Where'd you get the chopper?" Savage asked.

Silence.

"Um, we misappropriated it." Sinclair twisted around in her seat.

Savage raised an eyebrow.

"Hope that sheriff badge of yours has a get out of jail free card attached to it." Jed joked.

Sinclair sighed. "Let's just say, the guys at Sun Valley Farms are going to be mighty pissed we stole their crop duster."

Savage snorted. "It was for a worthy cause. We couldn't have gotten out of there without you."

"That's for sure," Thorpe agreed.

"I'll let you two explain that to them." Sinclair grinned at her colleagues.

"Where to?" asked Jed.

Sinclair nodded toward the back. "Given the state of these three, I think the nearest hospital."

The helicopter cleared the ridge and banked left, giving them all a view of the jagged rock face below. They soared over the valley, bypassing the sleeping town. Savage felt himself drifting off. The throbbing rotors and rushing air faded to a soft, soothing beat. The next thing he remembered was a team lifting him out of the helicopter and onto a stretcher at Durango General Hospital.

"We need to collect Jesse and Walker's bodies," he muttered to Sinclair, as he was wheeled away. They couldn't leave them on the mountain. Jesse deserved a proper burial, and there would be an investigation into both their deaths.

You'll never find them all.

Candy would testify that Walker had killed Jesse. As far as the investigation into Walker's death went, Candy would be cleared. No jury on earth would convict her, given what Walker had done.

"I'm on it." She gave him a thumbs up. He knew he could rest easy. Sinclair had everything under control.

SAVAGE'S NOSE TWITCHED. Was that Becca's perfume? Was she here?

He opened his eyes to find his fiancé sitting in the chair beside his hospital bed. "I thought that was you."

"Dalton." Her voice was soft. "Thank goodness you're okay."

"Of course I'm okay. Why wouldn't I be?"

She rolled her eyes. "I see you haven't lost your sense of humor."

"We got him," he said, as a fresh rush of pain made him grimace. At least his vision had cleared.

"Where does it hurt?" she asked.

He shook his head. Where didn't it hurt?

"The doctor said you had several fractures in your left hand, a concussion, bruised ribs, and he had to put stitches in that awful gash in your leg. It's going to leave a scar."

A scar was the least of his concerns.

"That it?"

She rolled her eyes.

He was more worried about his hand. Glancing down, he saw it wrapped in bandages, useless.

"You won't be able to drive for a while," she added. "It was pretty mashed up. What happened?" Her bright blue eyes were questioning.

"It's a long story."

"We have time."

He reached for her hand. "The guy we were chasing—"

"The serial killer, you mean?"

At his surprised look, she added, "I spoke to Thorpe."

He sighed and looked down at his hands. "Yeah, the serial killer. He stomped on it a couple of times."

"Is that when you got concussed?"

"No, that was before, when he got the jump on me. Although the rock smashing into my head probably didn't help either."

Her eyes widened. "Rock?"

"Yeah, but it's fine. I'm fine."

Her eyes narrowed.

"How's Thorpe?" He changed the subject.

"He's okay. Like you, he's got a couple of bruised ribs where Walker shot him in the vest, but he'll live. He's doing a lot better than you are."

Savage grunted. "That's good. At one point, we thought he was dead."

"I know." She squeezed his hand.

The pounding in Savage's head was deafening." He gazed at her gorgeous face. "You know, when I was lying up in the mountains, all I could think about was how I might not see you again, or our child." He shook his head at the memory. "I thought that was it, that Walker was going to use his last shot on me."

"But he didn't," she whispered.

Because there was no last shot. He suddenly felt emotional and turned his head away.

"We're fine," she told him. "Better than fine. While you were in the mountains, I thought of a name for our baby boy."

"You did?" He was grateful for the change in topic.

"Yeah. What do you think of Connor?"

"Connor." He rolled it off his tongue. "I like it. It's a strong name."

"I agree." She grinned at him.

"Connor it is."

It was while they were smiling at each other that Captain Birch stuck his head around the door.

"Sorry for the interruption. Can I have a word?"

"Yeah, I guess so." If only the pounding would ease a little. He glanced at Becca. "Can you find me some painkillers?"

"Sure." She smiled at Birch and left the ward. The Police Captain eased himself into the chair she'd vacated.

"It's good to see you," Birch began, his eyes crinkling. "I heard you had quite an adventure."

"You can say that again."

"Your deputies filled me in. I thought you'd like to know we found Walker's cabin. Less than two miles from where he attacked you at that outcrop."

Savage nodded, then wished he hadn't.

"Sniffer dogs had no problem finding it."

That made sense. They had access to Walker's backpack, and his body. The well-trained K9 unit would have sniffed out his trail, no problem at all.

"And?" Savage asked.

Birch sighed. "There were four different backpacks in there." He took off his cap and raked a hand through his hair, before putting it back on again. "Including one belonging to the missing twenty-one-year-old in New Mexico. It had her name on it."

"Mia," Savage whispered.

She was special. Took a long time to die.

Birch arched an eyebrow.

"He talked about her when he had me tied up. It was like he was gloating." A chill ran through him.

Birch shook his head.

"How many people do you think he's killed?" Savage asked. Walker was deranged. He enjoyed pounding his victims to death. Watching them as they died. Savage felt no remorse for the monster's death.

"A lot. In addition to the backpacks, we found some trinkets and other items of clothing, as well as a whole bunch of hiking paraphernalia. He had quite a collection going."

"Stuff he'd taken off his victims." Savage swallowed over the bitter taste in his mouth.

"Exactly. We've sent all of it to the lab for analysis. The DNA and fingerprints will hopefully tell us who it belongs to."

Savage gave a grim nod. The reality was, Walker had been doing this for a long time. "He told me we'd never find them all."

Birch's gaze turned cold. "He's right. We probably won't. But he favored the hiking trails, so that's a good place to start."

It wouldn't be easy. Savage didn't envy Birch his task.

"The FBI are taking over," he said, after a beat. Savage got the feeling he wasn't too happy about that. "They have more manpower. It'll be a joint task force."

Since Walker's bloody trail crossed state lines, it was only logical. The FBI had field offices all over and the resources to launch a massive investigation into the missing victims.

"Good luck," Savage said, leaning back on the pillow and closing his eyes.

Becca returned with the painkillers. "Here, the nurse said you can take two, but no more." She handed them to him with a glass of water.

With a groan, he knocked them back.

Birch stood up. "Feel better soon. We'll keep you posted."

"I'd appreciate that."

He tipped his cap to Becca as he left the ward.

"Have you seen Candy?" he asked his fiancé. "She's been through a hell of a lot in the last few days. I suspect she might need some trauma counseling."

"I did ask," she said, sitting down again. "But the nurse said she's gone."

"Gone?"

"Yeah, she checked herself out."

"What?" He struggled back up to a sitting position. "Does Birch know?"

"I don't know. Should I run after him?"

"No. If he doesn't know, he'll find out soon enough."

"What's the matter?" She frowned, worried.

"I just wanted to talk to her, make sure she was okay. Is Thorpe around?"

Becca stood up. "He's waiting outside. I'll send him in. I've got to get back to work, anyway."

"Becca?"

She gazed down at him. "Yeah?"

"I love you. I mean it."

Leaning over, she whispered, "I know. I love you too. Get some rest. I'll be back later."

Warmth spread through his tired, injured body as her lips touched his cheek. He felt absurdly grateful that she was in his life. If this experience had taught him anything, it was he'd never, ever take Becca for granted.

TWENTY-SIX

"YOU'RE POPULAR," Thorpe remarked, as he walked into the ward. "I've been waiting a while to see you."

Savage grinned. "It's good to see you, too."

Other than his pallor and multiple facial scratches from where he'd fought his way through the woodland, Thorpe was fully dressed and looking upbeat. For some reason, Savage didn't want to be stuck in the hospital bed anymore.

He folded back the covers. "Where are my clothes?"

"I'm not sure you should get up." The deputy glanced around for a nurse, but the ward was empty.

"I'm fine. Doc told me nothing was broken that couldn't heal." He'd had an update before Thorpe had been allowed in.

"What about your concussion?" Thorpe asked.

"It's mild. Scan was clear and my vision is back to normal."

"Okay then." Thorpe reached for the clothes Becca had brought, folded neatly on a duffle bag in the corner.

Savage pulled them on, then ran a hand through his hair, wincing as he touched the bumps. He had two, one at the back—compliments of the log Walker had hit him with—the other just above his temple from the rock. *Damn Walker.*

"How's Littleton?" Savage asked, as he bent down to pull on his shoes.

"He's recovering. Do you want to see him?"

"Yeah, let's go for a walk. I need to move before I stiffen up." He stood up slowly, holding onto the bed until he found his balance. The mauled thigh was tender, but nothing compared to the pain in his side, and the headache that had softened to a dull thump from the outright pounding. "Okay, let's go."

They took a slow walk down the hospital corridor. Thorpe kept glancing over to make sure Savage was okay. The more Savage walked, the better he felt.

"I'm good," he said, once they got to the end of the corridor. "Which way to Littleton's ward?"

"He's downstairs in the general ward," Thorpe told him.

They caught the elevator downstairs and navigated another long corridor before they reached Littleton's room. At first, Savage didn't see him, but then he spotted the slender deputy sitting up, reading a newspaper in a bed by the window.

Littleton had lost a lot of blood in the bear attack and was still under supervision, although Savage could tell by the color in his cheeks that he was making great strides.

"How are you feeling?" Savage perched on the end of the bed.

"I should be asking you that," Littleton retorted, then grinned. "I'm good. The doc says I can go home later today."

"That's great news," Thorpe said, standing behind Savage.

"I'm sorry I wasn't there to help take him down." Littleton hung his head. "I heard you could have used my help."

"You were injured," Savage pointed out. "It's not your fault. It's a miracle we got you off that mountain before you bled out. You did well to keep it together."

"Still, you guys went back up." His voice was filled with admiration. "I should have been there."

Savage shrugged. He didn't want the young deputy beating himself up about it. "I had no choice. Candy was still in the hands of that madman, not that we knew it at the time. Besides, Thorpe joined me, and we rescued her in the end."

"I heard what happened." Littleton shook his head. "I can't believe it. All those people. Sinclair told me what they'd found in the cabin."

"Where is Sinclair?" Savage asked. He wanted to thank her properly for stealing the helicopter and coming to get them.

"She's manning the station with Barbara."

That was to be expected. He could always count on Sinclair. For a moment, he thought about how the young deputy had become more like Hatch. Confident, fast-thinking, dependable. The veteran drifter had rubbed off on Sinclair.

"What happened to Candy?" Savage pulled his attention back to the woman they'd rescued. "Did you see her before she checked herself out?"

"No, but I heard the nurses talking." Littleton lowered his voice. "Apparently, she said she wasn't safe here, that they'd find her because it was all over the news."

Savage frowned. "Who'd find her?"

"I thought she was running from Jesse Turner," Thorpe said.

"So did I, but she seemed in fear for her life."

"You heard her say it wasn't safe?" Savage asked.

"No, but I spoke to the nurse. She told me Candy made quite the commotion. They had to let her go, since they couldn't keep her here against her will."

"And very definitely said they'd find her here, and that she wasn't safe?" Savage asked.

"Yeah." Littleton shrugged.

What the hell was she on about?

"We have to find her." He got to his feet. "There's something else going on."

"You mean something she hasn't told us?" Thorpe glanced between the two of them.

"Yeah, I'm getting a bad feeling. It was what Zeb said too. He told her to leave town until the heat died down. At the time I thought he meant Jesse, but now I'm not so sure." Zeb wouldn't have used that phrase to describe her ex-boyfriend.

"I'll come with you," Thorpe said. "You'll need someone to drive."

"I'll come too." Littleton threw back the covers.

"No, you stay put until the doc gives you the all-clear." Savage held up a hand. "It's only a couple hours. Then, if it's not too late, you can go into the station. I'm sure Sinclair could use your help."

"Yes, boss." His voice was firm. Littleton was eager to make up for his absence during the showdown in the mountains.

THEIR RECEPTION at the trailer park was different from last time. No glaring eyes following their every move, no stony glances, no hostile whispers. In fact, they even got a friendly wave from one of the residents tending her vegetable patch.

"Wow," said Thorpe, waving back. Word had clearly spread about Candy's rescue.

They parked outside of Candy's mother's house and knocked on the door. The man who'd been sleeping on the couch answered. "Yeah?"

"Is Martha here? We need to speak to her."

"No, she's at work. Won't be back until late."

"I'm Sheriff Savage, and this is Deputy Thorpe. Have you—?"

"I know who you are," the man drawled. "We're grateful that you found our Candy and brought her home safe."

Savage wasn't so sure the young woman would appreciate being called "our Candy" by her mother's boyfriend.

"Just doing our job, sir. Have you seen her since she's been back?"

"Yeah, but she didn't stay. Raced in to tell us she was alright, then raced straight out again. Upset her mama something terrible, she did."

"Did she say why she had to leave?" Savage asked.

"Nah, but it wasn't good. That girl was scared, I could tell."

Savage sighed, thanked him, and left the trailer. Outside, he turned to Thorpe. "Why do I get the feeling we're back to square one?"

"I'm confused." Thorpe scratched his head. "Why is she running? She didn't say anything to me about being scared."

"That's not too surprising."

"I guess so. Where would she go?" Thorpe frowned. "Surely not back up the mountain?"

"I doubt it." Savage tried to think as he gazed up and down the street. Zeb's Harley-Davidson glimmered outside his house, the chrome frame catching the late afternoon sun. "I have an idea. Wait here."

Ignoring the throbbing in his side, he strolled across the street.

Zeb opened the door before he got there. "Jeez, man. What happened to you?"

"Long story. You seen Candy?"

A sigh. "Not this again."

"I'm afraid so. She's gone missing."

"Thought you found her and brought her back. Rescued her from some madman in the mountains." He shot his old colleague an admiring glance. "Always the hero, hey Dalton?"

There was a tinge of resentment in Zeb's tone, but Savage wasn't going to get into it. Old wounds were best forgotten. "I do my best." Savage paused. "She's gone again. Why do you think that is, Zeb?"

"How the hell should I know?"

Savage studied the other man. He could tell his old colleague was lying. It was in the way his eyes shifted when he spoke. He'd seen it when he'd questioned Zeb about the evidence he'd claimed he hadn't stolen from the lockers back in Denver, and he saw it now. "Where is she, Zeb?"

"I told you, I don't know."

"Come on. Nothing happens around here without you noticing."

Zeb said nothing, holding Savage's gaze. That much was true. Here, Zeb was master of his domain. Savage wondered if the residents of the trailer park knew their landlord used to be a cop. "That's true, isn't it?"

"You know me too well, Dalton." Zeb threw up his hands.

"I'm waiting."

"Okay, but don't go spreading it around." Zeb lowered his voice to a hoarse whisper. "She's holed up at Jesse's brother's place."

Savage stared at him. "Blake Turner? Why'd she go there? I'd have thought she'd want nothing to do with Jesse's family."

"Jesse isn't the problem here," he said wryly. "Never was."

Savage rubbed his forehead. "I wish someone would just tell me what the heck is going on."

"Let's go inside. Don't want anyone to see me talking to you."

Savage gestured to Thorpe to wait and followed the ex-cop into his house.

"Nice place you got here," he commented, glancing around. The mobile home was spacious, but cozy. A damn sight better than the apartment Zeb had owned in Denver.

"I like it." Zeb gestured for Savage to sit.

"Let's just get to it," Savage said. There was no time to waste. If Candy was in trouble, he wanted to know.

"It all started last week at the biker bar where she works," Zeb said, lighting up a cigarette. Savage remembered Zeb used to take a lot of smoke breaks on the job.

"The Roadhouse?"

"Yeah. It was after that bank heist in Durango."

Savage frowned, remembering. "Five hundred thousand dollars."

"That's the one. Audacious heist. Broad daylight. Four guys, in and out in less than five minutes."

"How'd you know so much about it?" Savage's eyes narrowed.

Zeb shrugged. "I pay attention."

Savage was beginning to connect the dots. "And this heist was connected to the biker bar?"

"That is not for me to say. But..." Zeb paused for effect. "Candy said three guys came in that afternoon and started celebrating. She heard them mention the money."

"The five hundred grand?" Savage's eyebrows shot up.

"Yeah. Problem was, Axle clocked her. He went after her and she ran. That's all I know."

"Axle?"

"He runs the Crimson Angels. Big, hairy bastard, got a thing for skulls."

Savage contemplated this for a while. "Candy must have been pretty convinced they were involved to disappear like that."

"I advised her to get out of town, to go to the mountains, anywhere. Just until things settled down. Said I'd talk to Axle about it, try to smooth things over."

"And did you?" Savage asked.

"No, man. I tried, but he wasn't in a talkative mood. Warned me to stay out of it." Zeb shook his head. "I'm not getting involved in any shit, man. I like living here. I don't need to get on the wrong side of the Crimson Angels."

"Standing up for what's right as usual," Savage muttered.

"Hey, man. I could get shot for telling you this."

Savage held up a hand. "Okay, okay. I understand. If these guys were responsible, things could get messy." Savage had heard of the Crimson Angels. They were a trouble-causing biker gang. A veritable army. And not one he particularly wanted to cross.

"I hope you find her," Zeb said. "She's a good kid."

Savage tensed his jaw. "So do I."

TWENTY-SEVEN

BLAKE TURNER STOOD outside his house with a shotgun as Savage and Thorpe pulled into the driveway. "Zeb must have called ahead," Savage surmised. "Given him a heads up."

"If you're looking for Jesse, my brother's dead," Blake called, a catch in his voice.

Savage climbed out of the car. "I know. I'm sorry for your loss." Beside him, Thorpe held his hands where Blake could see them. They could hear the same dog barking in the background.

"We just wanna talk," Savage said. "We're looking for Candy."

"What do you want with her?" He didn't say she wasn't here, or he hadn't seen her.

"I want to check up on her," Savage said. "She's been through a traumatic ordeal." Savage left out that she'd killed a man. Candy may not have told Blake what had happened.

"I know."

A shadow appeared at the window overlooking the front porch. Savage recognized the blonde hair. "I know she's here, Blake. You let us talk to her and we'll leave you alone."

He hesitated, but the front door opened, and Candy appeared.

"You okay with this?" Blake asked her.

"Yeah, let them in."

Jesse's brother stood aside and let Savage and Thorpe walk past him. Once they were inside the house, Blake kept up the vigil outside.

"You expecting someone?" Savage asked, closing the door behind them.

Candy gave him a scared look. "Maybe." She was as jittery as a cicada.

"Zeb told me about what happened at the Roadhouse."

Her eyes widened. "What did he tell you? He doesn't know anything."

"He knows a couple biker thugs are after you," Thorpe pointed out.

Candy sighed, her gaze softening as she looked at Thorpe. "I told him that much."

Thorpe gestured to the sofa. Savage was happy to let his deputy take control of the situation. Candy liked him, so Thorpe had the advantage here. "What happened, Candy? Why are these guys after you?"

She bit her lip, unsure how to proceed. Savage thought how different she looked from when he'd last seen her. She was clean, for one. Her hair straighter and glossier than he remembered, and she wore track pants and a pink T-shirt with a sparkly heart on it. On her feet were tennis shoes, but underneath, she'd have stitches.

"If you tell us, we might be able to help you," Savage said.

She sank onto the sofa. "Nobody can help me. I'm in a lot of trouble."

"Try us," Savage said.

She glanced at them both, then gave a tiny nod. "I was working at the Roadhouse when these two guys walked in. They were all excited and pumped up. I served them a couple beers, didn't take much notice, and moved on to the next customer."

"Go on." Thorpe sat down next to her. Savage remained by the door, where he had a good view of the front of the house. Blake paced up and down the porch with his shotgun. They could hear his boots on the wooden timbers as he walked.

"Then this mean-looking biker dude came in and told them to quiet down. I recognized him from the Crimson Angels, although he doesn't live in Hawk's Landing. Maybe Durango." She shrugged. "One of the three said, 'but it's five hundred thousand dollars.'"

"He said that?" Savage asked. "He mentioned five hundred thousand dollars?"

"Yeah, I heard clear as day. The mean dude got angry and told the other guy to shut up, then my boss Axle came over. He owns the bar. I tried to make out like I hadn't heard anything, but he wasn't buying it." She caught her breath. "The way he looked at me, I knew I was in trouble."

"What did you do?" asked Thorpe.

"I hauled ass to the ladies' and climbed out the window, that's what. I wasn't gonna hang around and get strung up by a bunch of biker thugs. I know how they shut people up. It's not pretty."

"You went to Zeb for help?" Savage guessed.

"Yeah, he told me to leave town for a few days and he'd handle it." She glanced at her hands. "I had nowhere to go, so I took to the mountains. I love it up there." Pausing, she swallowed. "Or I used to."

Thorpe put his hand over hers, and she offered him a watery smile. "You will again."

She shook her head. "I don't ever want to walk those trails again. Not after what happened. It'll never be the same again."

"Did anyone else know where you were going?" Savage asked.

"Only Zeb, and he said he'd tell Jesse."

"Jesse?" Thorpe stared at her.

Savage shook his head, confused. "Jesse knew where you were going?"

"Yeah, he was coming to help me. Zeb told him what had happened, and he was furious. He set off after me, but..." She faded off. "You know the rest."

"That's why Jesse shot out of here like a bat out of hell," Savage murmured. "It wasn't because he was angry with you?"

"No, we'd put all that testimony crap behind us. Jesse forgave me. He knew he was in the wrong. In fact, he was turning over a new leaf. Ask Blake, he'll tell you."

"We did," Savage muttered, thinking how different his approach would have been if he'd known Jesse was there to help Candy, not hunt her down. Then again, they might never have gone up the mountain, discovered Mark Stillwell's body, or realized Candy had been kidnapped by a rock-wielding maniac. A twinge of pain shot through his broken hand at the memory. "What did Zeb mean when he said he'd handle it?"

She tossed her hair back off her shoulder. "I don't know. Talk to them, I guess. He used to ride with them. Did you know that?"

"I did," Savage said.

She nodded. "But I don't think it worked. They came to my mama's trailer last night, beat up Austin."

"Who's Austin?" Thorpe frowned.

"The guy my mama's seeing. He's okay, apart from the weed. I mean, he treats her right."

And the whores, thought Savage.

"What about you?" Thorpe asked. "Does he treat you right?"

She didn't quite meet his gaze. "I have my own place now, above the Roadhouse. Or I did." Tears filled her eyes.

Thorpe shot Savage a knowing look. "They'll stake out the place in case she returns."

He gave a grim nod. "We can protect you, Candy."

"How?" Her voice wobbled. "These guys know who I am. I've testified against someone before. They're not going to take that risk with me. I can identify them in a line-up."

"Would you?" Savage asked. "If we got enough evidence to bring them in."

"There are too many of them," she whispered. "I know how these guys operate. They'll keep coming after me. If not those ones, then others. It's never going to end." She stifled a sob.

"We might want to put her in WITSEC," Thorpe suggested.

Savage was nodding slowly. "I'll make a deal with you, Candy. You help us get them, and we'll make sure no one ever hurts you again."

"You're going to send me away?" Her voice was small.

"A new start," Thorpe said. "You said yourself you didn't want to step foot in these mountains again. How about new mountains? A new life? Somewhere you can start over."

She thought about that for a while, then nodded. "I could do that."

"Good." Savage moved away from the window. "We'll have to take you into police custody for now, just until we sort this out. You'll be safer that way. Then once you've identified the suspects, we'll make you disappear."

"What about my things?" Her eyes were huge, teary.

"Give Thorpe a list and he'll get them for you."

She sniffed. "Okay, thanks."

They got up to leave when they heard Blake give a loud whistle. Savage strode to the window and looked out. "Oh, hell. That's not good."

"What's happening?" Thorpe asked.

A cloud of dust rolled up the driveway, accompanied by a low rumble. Motorbikes, and lots of them.

Candy ran up beside them, her face ashen. She clutched Thorpe's arm. "They're here. They've found me."

TWENTY-EIGHT

THE CRIMSON ANGELS swarmed up the driveway, the collective roar of their motorcycles amplified as they drew nearer.

Candy backed away from the window, her eyes huge. "What are we gonna do?"

Blake ran into the house and bolted the door behind him. "We've got trouble."

Savage turned to Thorpe. "Get her out of here."

"Use the side door," Blake said. "You can leave through the garage that way."

Thorpe gave a stiff nod.

Candy glanced at Blake, stricken. "There's nothing out here except fields and mountains."

"You've got to go now," Savage said. "Once they surround the house, it'll be too late."

Thorpe took Candy's hand.

"Use the dirt bike," Blake said.

The deputy broke into a grin. "You have a dirt bike?"

"Yeah, a 250xc. I used to race. Here." He fished in his pocket and tossed the set of keys to Thorpe.

Candy's eyes lit up. "If we cut across the field, we can use the lower trails behind the park to get away."

"Good idea." Thorpe turned to Savage. "You sure about this? I don't like leaving you." Last time he'd done that, things hadn't worked out so well.

"We'll be okay. They want Candy. The best thing you can do is get her out of here."

The deputy nodded, then turned to Candy. "Let's go."

They ran through the house to the garage door. Savage heard it slam shut but couldn't hear the dirt bike splutter to life over the din of approaching Harleys. He took a deep breath and looked at Blake. "It's probably best if you let me do the talking."

Blake nodded, pale beneath his tan.

"You stay here in case I need backup."

Blake shook his shotgun in reply.

Savage waited until he was certain Thorpe and Candy had gone, then drew his weapon and went outside. He stood on the porch and watched the cacophony of Harleys come to a stop. Dust swirled as the gang dismounted and removed their helmets. Twelve in total. A bit excessive, in his opinion.

A long-haired, grizzly bear of a man in full leathers approached the house.

"That's close enough." Savage held up his silver star.

The man stopped. A silver skull pendant on the chain around his neck glinted as it caught the light. "We don't want no trouble. We just want to talk to Candy Ray."

"Candy's not here."

The two men scowled at each other.

"Where is she?" the biker asked.

"That's none of your concern," Savage replied.

"I have business to discuss with her."

"Is that right? What kind of business would that be?"

The biker hesitated. "That's nothing to do with you."

"It wouldn't be illegal business, would it?" Savage asked, trying his best to be polite.

"No, sir."

"Then you won't mind telling me what it is."

A longer pause. The biker looked around. "We could shoot you and search the place ourselves, just to make sure you're not lying."

"You could," Savage agreed. "But you'd be shooting the County Sheriff, which means spending the rest of your days behind bars. Not to mention breaking and entering, trespassing on private property, intimidation." He paused. "Should I go on?"

The biker glared at Savage. The moment dragged on. Eventually, the biker made a spinning gesture in the air with his finger, and the gang climbed back onto their bikes.

"We know she's been staying here," the biker said. "We'll be back."

"I hope not," Savage called after them. "Anything happens to that girl, and I'll know who to look for."

He watched as they restarted their machines and turned around, kicking up more dust as they took off back down the road.

"THAT'S HIM." Savage pointed to a mugshot of the big, bearded guy. The AC in the sheriff's department had been cranked up to cool the room down. It was too warm for a spring day, not a cloud in the sky. Hard to believe that just yesterday, it was pouring down rain on the east-facing slope of the mountain.

Savage still felt like he had a layer of dust sticking to him, thanks to the Crimson Angels and their mini dust storm.

"You sure?" Sinclair asked, operating the computer.

"No doubt about it." Savage had pulled up a chair next to her. "He's aged a few years, but that's him."

"Axle Weston," she read. "Real name: Harold Gaywood."

"I can see why he changed it."

"He's got an impressive rap sheet." She raised an eyebrow. "Disturbing the peace, drug dealing, running girls, and racketeering. He served two years for possession."

"When was that?" Savage squinted at the small font on the screen.

"Eight years ago at Crowley County Correctional. Hasn't been back since."

"He either got smarter or he's keeping his nose clean," Barbara chimed in, scooting her chair out from behind the desk.

"I'm betting the former." Sinclair rolled her eyes. "People like that don't change. It's not in their nature."

"Judging by what happened this afternoon, I have to agree." Savage leaned back and folded his arms. "I'm going to pay Zeb another visit. I'm sure he's holding back."

"I'll drive you." Sinclair said. His crushed hand put him out of commission for at least a month. "Doctor's orders."

He pulled a face. "Thanks."

"You visiting that ex-cop you told me about? The one that runs the trailer park now?"

"That's right. We served together in Denver. Saved my life." He didn't know why he'd added that. Perhaps to justify why he'd ever talk to Zeb in the first place.

Sinclair gawked at him. "You'll have to tell us about that."

"It's a story for another day." He got up and grabbed his jacket. "See you tomorrow, Barbara. I'm gonna head home after this, spend some time with Becca."

"You do that." Barbara smiled. "You deserve some time with her, after that adventure in the mountains."

He flexed his injured hand and grimaced. "Don't remind me."

"Where's Candy now?" Sinclair asked, as she grabbed her keys.

"Thorpe's got her in a no-tell motel. She'll be okay there until we can figure out what to do next."

"Are you planning to put her in WITSEC?" Barbara had been speaking to Thorpe on the phone.

"I'll give them a call if it comes to that. Let's see what Axle Weston and his crew are up to first. If we can bust them for the Durango heist, we'll need her to testify."

"Poor girl's been through so much," Barbara mused.

"She's a toughie." Savage pursed his lips. "I think she'll be just fine."

SINCLAIR DROVE them back to the trailer park.

"Can't stay away, huh?" Zeb said, once he'd opened the door to them.

"So it would seem." Savage walked straight past him into the house.

"Please, come in," Zeb quipped, following him in. Sinclair came in behind them.

"You may as well have a seat. Can I get you anything?"

"No thanks, we won't be here long enough."

Zeb nodded. "What can I help you with this time, Dalton?"

"Axle Weston."

Zeb's gaze narrowed. "I told you, I'm not getting on the wrong side of him."

"Just want to know what you know about him."

Zeb sighed. "I can't say much, you understand. If he found out I was talking to you, there'd be a hell of a shitstorm coming my way."

"I understand, but anything you can tell us would help."

Zeb shrugged. "You know the type. Into a lot of different trouble. From what I heard, the guy rocked up about a decade ago from out of nowhere and took over as President of the Crimson Angels. The previous President went down for twenty-five years for shooting someone. Don't ask me who, I wasn't around back then."

"When last did you see him?" Savage asked. A scantily clad woman with dark hair and smudged lips sauntered through the living room on her way to the kitchen. She gave Savage a provocative smile.

"What are you doing here, Loretta?" Zeb barked. "I told you never to come into the house when I had company."

Sinclair arched an eyebrow. The lady was clearly one of his 'employees'.

"You said I could grab some coffee after my shift." She pouted.

He waved her on. "Hurry up."

She continued on her way.

"Mixing business with pleasure?" Savage asked, knowingly.

"Loretta's my niece," Zeb replied, although they all knew he was lying.

"Nice outfit," Sinclair remarked dryly.

Zeb didn't respond. "What was I saying?"

"You were about to tell me when you last saw Axle Weston," Savage reminded him.

"Well, I saw him this afternoon, not long after you left."

"What a coincidence." Savage had guessed as much. "You tell him where Candy was, too?"

Zeb shrugged. "I knew you'd get her out of there before he got near the place. Saw no point in pissin' the guy off."

"And getting kicked out of the club," Savage muttered.

"I'm not in the club," Zeb said quickly. "I'm what they call a hang around, not a patched member. I have nothing to do with club affairs. I just like to go on rides occasionally."

"Uh-huh," Savage muttered, not sure if he believed him. "I wouldn't want to arrest you for association."

"What do you mean by arrest? You talking about that bank heist?"

"If you know anything," Savage said. "Now's the time to tell us."

Zeb walked over to a liquor cabinet and unscrewed a bottle of whisky. "Want one?"

"No thanks."

Sinclair shook her head.

"I heard rumors, like everyone else." The whisky tinkled as it hit the glass. "Nothing concrete. Three guys partying it up at the Roadhouse."

"They stole five hundred thousand dollars." Savage had checked with the bank in Durango.

"I don't know anything about that."

"What? Candy didn't tell you about the money?"

Zeb shook his head. "I used to be a cop, Dalton. Some things people won't tell me, and to be honest, I don't wanna know."

Savage gave him a hard look. "That didn't stop you before."

"Now, hold on a minute. That was never proven—"

Savage held up a hand. "Forget it. It's in the past. If you do hear anything, you'll let me know, okay?"

"Sure." Zeb looked sulky. Like hell, he'd let the cops know if he heard anything. He wasn't a fool. He'd keep it to himself or use it for his own benefit. Savage knew exactly what Zeb was like.

"See ya, Zeb, and a word of advice."

Zeb glanced up.

"Next time, keep your girls under wraps. There are some things I don't wanna see either."

TWENTY-NINE

"WHAT WAS NEVER PROVEN?" Sinclair asked the moment they climbed back into the car. They were driving the Crown Vic since Thorpe had the Suburban.

"Ten kilos of cocaine went missing from police lockup," Savage explained, leaning his head back against the headrest. "They never found out who took it, and after that, they installed cameras in the evidence room."

"You think it was Zeb?"

Savage shrugged. "Like he said, it was never proven."

"Is that why he left the Force?"

"Yeah. Internal Affairs made a stink about it, and he accused them of targeting him. He wasn't the most popular detective."

"I wonder why," she mused.

"Anyway, he left after that. Came down here, bought the trailer park, and has been living off the rental ever since. He runs girls on the side, but it's a decent establishment. He doesn't allow drugs, the girls are clean, and he provides a service to the local area. I figure unless there's any harm done, it's not worth the hassle."

Sinclair gave him a sideways look. "You feel like you owe him, don't you? For saving your life."

"He's a useful informant."

"Will you tell me what happened?"

Savage picked up his cellphone. "Sure, just let me make a call."

He dialed the Durango sheriff's office. "Hudson, it's Dalton Savage. I've got a lead on your bank heist."

He told him about the bikers partying at the Roadhouse. "One of the bar staff heard them mention five hundred thousand. Yeah, for real. I've got a name for you if you wanna organize a raid. Axle Weston, head of the Crimson Angels. Based here in Hawk's Landing."

After he hung up, Sinclair said, "What are you hoping to find? They won't have stashed the loot at the chief's house."

"I know. Just thought I'd send him a message," Savage gave a half grin.

"You're stirring up the hornet's nest. He'll know it was you."

"Good. Maybe he'll think twice before going after Candy."

"I hope you're right." Sinclair put the car in gear and drove out of the trailer park. The sky was a pale blue above them, not a cloud in sight. Country and western music played softly on the radio.

"You gonna tell me the story?" Sinclair glanced over at him.

"If I have to."

"I'd like to hear it."

He sighed. "I'd just been transferred to homicide. My partner and I responded to a call to help the Denver Police Department Fugitive Unit arrest a suspect near a shopping mall. He was wanted for shooting another man in the face after a parking dispute."

Sinclair shook her head without taking her eyes off the road.

"An off-duty officer saw him go into the mall and radioed it in. We were the first unit to arrive on the scene. We hid in the bushes, ready to ambush him. Chances were, he was still armed."

"What happened?"

"As he came out, my partner used a flashbang grenade to divert his attention. While he was confused, I tried to arrest him. I told him to raise his hands, but he fled to a car and jumped inside, pushing the pregnant mother out of the way."

Sinclair bit her lip.

"I helped the woman up, but by that time, the suspect had pulled out a pistol and aimed it at me through the car window."

"What did you do?" she whispered.

"I shielded the woman and backed away, but my partner came running up. Spooked, the suspect shot my partner and then turned the gun back to me."

She gasped.

"I only took a flesh wound, but my partner went down. I laid on the ground on top of this woman, praying he wouldn't take another shot at us."

Sinclair was hanging onto every word.

"The guy was on a roll. He fired but couldn't get the right angle out of the car window, and it hit the tarmac next to us. The woman started screaming. He took aim again, leaning further out of the window. I was convinced that was it. Game over."

Sinclair whistled under her breath.

"Then I heard gunfire and the sound of glass breaking and when I looked up, I saw the fugitive leaning over the steering wheel."

"Zeb?" Sinclair guessed.

"Yeah, he shot the guy in the head," Savage said. "He'd arrived in a squad car and approached from the other side. We didn't know he was there." He paused, reflecting. "If Zeb hadn't taken that shot, that would have been it for me." He gave a little shake of his head.

"And the pregnant woman," Sinclair added.

"Yup."

"Zeb saved your life."

"Yeah, and I've never forgotten it."

BECCA'S FACE lit up as Savage walked into the house. She had that healthy glow everyone talked about. Pregnancy agreed with her. "How are you feeling?"

"Good. Now that the morning sickness is over, I'm feeling great."

"Sure you're not overdoing it?"

"I'm pregnant, Dalton. Not sick."

"I know, I know." He walked to the coffee pot to pour himself a brew, feeling a little embarrassed. Of course she was fine. This was Becca they were talking about. He'd never known her not to be fine.

She came up behind him. "But I like that you're worried about me." She smiled. "It makes a change."

He couldn't resist a wry grin. "It does, doesn't it?"

Taking his bandaged hand in hers, she asked, "How are you?"

"Okay." At least it wasn't his gun hand. "Not driving is a pain."

"Thorpe's a good driver."

"I know, but he's safeguarding Candy right now. Sinclair's been carting me around." He hated relying on others, even though they were a team.

"How is Becky? I haven't seen her since..." She frowned. "Forever."

"She's good. Learned a lot from Hatch. Her progress has been amazing."

"That's good." Becca didn't bring up Hatch as a rule. She knew of their history, but also that it was behind him. At one point, he'd been in love with Hatch, but after she left town, he'd thought that was it for him. Becca had made him realize he could love again. Now he couldn't imagine being with anyone else. Clever, calm, and intuitive, Becca was the perfect antidote to his high-stakes, frenetic existence.

Picking up his coffee, he nudged her over to the table where they both sat down.

"Long day?"

"You have no idea." The coffee was good, and he closed his eyes. It felt good to block out the world, if only for an instant. All he could feel was her hand on his arm.

"Tell me," Becca said, getting comfortable.

"What? You also just got home."

"I've been back awhile. I finished early today."

"Everything alright?" He frowned.

"Yes, of course, everything's fine. I'd tell you if it wasn't."

He gave an uncertain nod.

"I'm listening." Her voice was soft. "What's going on?"

After a sip of coffee, he filled her in, starting with the bank heist in Durango. Then the three bikers dropping cash like there was no tomorrow, Candy's attempted escape, and the face-to-face with Axle at Blake Turner's house.

"You think they did it?" she asked. "This biker club?"

"A couple members of it, yeah. It's gotta be them. His crew are too thick to not go spending what they stole. The bills were marked, so when they do, we'll pick 'em up."

"What about Candy?" Becca said. "You're worried about her, aren't you?"

"Yeah, but she'll be okay. After she testifies, we'll put 'em away and she can get on with her life."

"Those bikers have long memories," she said.

He raised an eyebrow. "What do you know about that?"

She shrugged. "This is Colorado. Everybody knows that."

"Hmm." He studied her. Had she just evaded the question?

"Okay." She threw her hands in the air. "I used to date a biker. It was a long time ago. During my wild phase."

"You had a wild phase?" He pretended to be shocked.

"Yeah." She flushed. "You don't know everything about me."

He squeezed her hand playfully. "Evidently."

She laughed.

"Okay, I won't pry into your wild past, but I've got one question."

"Okay." Her forehead furrowed. "What's that?"

"Which club did he ride with, this boyfriend of yours?"

She scrunched up her eyes, remembering. "The Hellcats. Back when I lived in Boulder." He remembered her saying she'd grown up there.

Not related then. "I can't picture you as a biker chick."

"I can dig out my leather jacket if you like."

He chuckled. "Now *that* I'd like to see."

Just as things were getting interesting, his phone rang. He shot her an apologetic look and answered, "Savage."

"Dalton, this is Zeb. Marshall Sullivan's at my place, throwing one helluva party. Just thought you might like to know."

Marshal Sullivan was one of Axle Weston's associates and a fellow member of the Crimson Angels. He was one of the three men Candy said she'd seen in the Roadhouse talking about the money.

"Thanks, Zeb," he said. "I'll be right over."

THIRTY

"SORRY TO GET YOU UP," Savage said when Sinclair picked him up in her cruiser. He hated not being able to drive himself around.

"I was awake anyway," she told him, with a sideways grin.

Classic rock music played on the radio as they drove to the Hidden Gem trailer park. "How's your hand?" Sinclair asked.

"Getting there, slowly." He flexed it, the fingers stiff and unyielding. "Doc said not to drive for three weeks, but I'm hoping it'll be sooner than that."

Patience was not his strong suit.

They drove through the open gates, bouncing over the uneven ground until they got to the dirt road that weaved through the trailer park. There was hardly anyone around. A group of teenagers sat on a porch, their faces eerily lit by their phone screens. A lone man got out of his car. A cat slunk across the road in front of them, its eyes luminous in the darkness.

Sinclair pulled over outside Zeb's house. His motorcycle was nowhere to be seen, and no lights were on through the windows.

"He must be out," she said.

Convenient. "Zeb won't want Marshall to know he's the one who called it in."

They heard the screeching and laughter as soon as they got out of the cruiser. It reached them easily over the unmistakable twang of an electric guitar track. "It's coming from behind the trees." Sinclair cocked her head to the side.

A row of dark, shadowy pines loomed behind the house. "That's where the trailers are."

She glanced over at Savage.

"It's where Zeb's 'niece' and her two friends conduct business."

Her eyes widened in understanding. There was a loud splash, followed by a volley of giggles.

"Was that water?" Sinclair asked. "It's a bit late for a pool party."

"Let's go." Savage drew his firearm and headed around the back. Sinclair followed a step behind. A blow-up swimming pool was filled to the brim and a butt-naked Marshall sat inside, splashing around with three equally naked young women. He reminded Savage of an overgrown kid in a paddling pool.

A cooler of beer stood to one side, along with an assortment of female clothing strewn over the lawn. They were having such a good time, they didn't even notice the two law enforcement officers barging in.

"Sorry to interrupt the party," Savage said, after a long moment had passed. He flashed his badge. "Can we have a word, Marshall?"

Sinclair had snuck to the other side of the pool and stood motionless, her gun in her hand.

"What the—" The biker turned around, surprised at the interruption. His eyes flitted from Savage to Sinclair and back again. "What you guys doing here?"

"Get out of the pool."

"Why? I ain't done nothing wrong." Water dripped off the hairy guy's beard. His wet, slicked back hair emphasized his receding hairline. Tattoos covered his biceps and furry chest, but soaking wet and without the leather jacket and combat boots, he didn't look so badass.

"That remains to be seen," Savage quipped. "Right now, I want to ask you some questions."

Glaring at them, Marshall climbed out of the swimming pool, giving them a full-frontal exposé.

"Oh, Lord," groaned Sinclair. Marshall was too angry to hear her.

Savage motioned to the women. "Ladies, if you wouldn't mind giving us some privacy." The three girls scuttled out of the pool and disappeared inside the house, not bothering to pick up their clothes. They were more concerned with the presence of law enforcement than their nakedness.

"What is it?" Marshall stepped towards his clothes, a messy pile next to his motorcycle. Black jeans, black T-shirt, worn leather jacket. A wallet bulging with bills had been tossed on top. Payment for the next few hours of fun.

"Oh, no you don't." Savage gestured for him to stay where he was. There'd be a weapon buried underneath those clothes. Guys like Marshall Sullivan didn't go anywhere unarmed. "Keep your hands where I can see them."

The biker shot daggers at them but stayed where he was. Sinclair kept her eyes glued to his face and her gun level with his chest.

"What's this about, Sheriff?"

"I want to know where you got the money from." Savage watched Marshall's face while Sinclair kept her hand steady.

"What money?" He feigned innocence. "A man's allowed to have a good time."

"These girls cost money," Savage said. "Money I know you don't have."

"Who says?"

"Your bank manager, Marshall. Come on, now. Where'd you get the cash?"

Marshall glanced at the ground. "I took on some extra work."

"Yeah? Where?"

"At the Roadhouse."

"You waiting tables now?" Savage smirked, knowing it would rile the biker. Even Sinclair managed a weak smile.

They got a sulky response. "I'm not at liberty to say."

"Oh, should I ask Axle then? I'm sure your boss will be very interested to hear what you've been up to."

Panic flickered across Marshall's face. Savage had heard that Axle ruled the Crimson Angels with an iron fist. There was an unhealthy level of fear and respect there, probably because he was the brains of the outfit. None of the others could outsmart him. Savage had heard some horrific stories about those who'd tried. Rumor had it that one of the bar staff who'd been caught skimming had his finger cut off with a pair of wire cutters. The guy was walking around with half a pinkie.

Who knew if it was true or not? It didn't really matter. The guy was scum, as far as he was concerned. Little more than a thug with a bike.

"I wonder what he'll say when he finds out you've been down here enjoying yourself." Savage knew he'd hit a nerve.

"Don't do that," Marshall begged. "He'll kill me."

"Well then?" Savage waited for the big man to answer. Marshall was thinking hard, trying to come up with something plausible.

"The truth is always the easiest option," Savage pointed out. "It requires less forethought."

"I told you, I've been doing some odd jobs." Marshall's face went blank, he was shutting down. Savage recognized the signs. Defense mode. Fear of his boss was stronger than his fear of law enforcement. "Running errands, that sort of thing."

"Robbing banks?" Savage asked.

Marshall couldn't hide his knee-jerk reaction. "Heck, no! Why would you ask that?"

"Oh, I don't know. Maybe because you're here, having your own private party after you were seen flashing money around the Roadhouse?"

"Hey, I wasn't involved in that heist, man. I swear I was nowhere near Durango that night. You ask my friends. They'll vouch for me."

"Yeah, about twenty friends," Savage said. "I'll bet they'll all swear you were with them the afternoon of the bank robbery."

Marshall's offended expression was prize-worthy. "I was."

"Yeah right." Savage sighed. They weren't going to make any leeway tonight. Marshall wasn't going to rat out his boss. He turned to Sinclair. "Let's confiscate Marshall's things here. Save us searching him once he puts them on."

"No, wait." He made a beeline for his clothes, but Savage raised his gun. "I wouldn't if I were you. Not if you're going for your weapon."

The hairy biker froze in the running man position.

"Deputy, if you wouldn't mind?"

Sinclair holstered her weapon and pulled on a pair of forensic gloves. Then she set about collecting Marshall's clothes along with his wallet, belt, and shoes.

"You can't do that," the biker wailed.

"I think you'll find we can." Savage gave him a hard look. "We're investigating a bank robbery and right now, you're our prime suspect."

Sinclair put the items in a large black bag.

"What about my clothes?" he wailed.

"You'll get them back. Eventually."

"I mean, what am I supposed to wear now?" He tried to cover himself with his hands. If it wasn't so late and he wasn't so tired, Savage would have found the situation funny.

"That's not my problem." He turned on his heel. "Sinclair, let's go."

They strode back to their vehicle, leaving the biker wearing nothing but a look of horror.

Once in the car, Sinclair chuckled. "Now that's a sight I'm not going to forget in a hurry."

Savage allowed himself a small grin. "Can you take that back to the station and log it as evidence? We'll go through his pockets tomorrow and see if any of the notes match the ones from the bank. In the meantime, I'm going home to Becca."

"Sure thing, boss." She started the car and reversed out of Zeb's driveway. "I'll drop you off."

THIRTY-ONE

"ANY LUCK WITH THOSE BANK NOTES?" Savage asked, as he strode into the station the next morning. Becca had left early for work, although she was winding down now and wasn't taking on any new patients. Another few months, and she'd be on maternity leave.

He caught his breath. It wouldn't be long before their lives changed forever. Baby Connor would be with them before they knew it, and not just as a bump in his fiancé's stomach, but a real-life squirming, crying baby—and what little he knew about newborns was dangerous.

Swallowing the anticipation, he put the thought out of his mind. He wasn't here to daydream.

Barbara poked her head out of her office. "Sinclair's not in yet, but she did check them into evidence late last night. I saw the logbook this morning."

"Okay, fine. It can wait."

Knowing Sinclair, she wouldn't be much later. She, Thorpe, and Littleton were all punctual. He felt a surge of pride. They were a good team. Just look at what they'd accomplished, despite the obvious drawbacks of age and experience. They'd apprehended a serial killer, rescued Candy, and were on their way to solving a bank heist.

Speaking of Candy, he wondered how she was doing. He called Thorpe at the motel. The deputy answered on the first ring.

"How's our witness doing?"

"All good here." Thorpe sounded spritely. "No trouble so far."

"Let's hope it stays that way. How are you two getting along?"

There was a slight pause. "Fine."

Savage smiled to himself. "Keep up the good work. We know Axle Weston and his boys want her out of the way, so stay vigilant."

"Will do. What's the news on the case? Anything I can do from here? I have my laptop with me." Thorpe didn't go anywhere without his laptop.

"One of the Crimson Angels, Marshall Sullivan, was partying up a storm at Zeb's last night," Savage told him. "We confiscated a wad of cash from his wallet. We'll compare it to the serial numbers from the bank job."

"Let's hope they match. I wanna nail these bastards."

"Yeah, likewise."

"Did you speak to him?" Thorpe asked.

"Yeah, but he didn't give anything away. He's got an alibi for the time of the robbery—he was out riding with his biker buddies. We have no way of disproving it. Those guys are tight. They'll vouch for each other. We won't get anything out of them."

"I reviewed the Durango Sheriff's report on the heist," Thorpe said.

Savage was impressed. He'd been meaning to do that but hadn't had the chance. "And?"

"There were several people in the bank at the time. Scared out of their minds from the gunshots, but almost all of them remember seeing four bank robbers."

"Any ID?" Savage asked, even though he knew witness accounts were notoriously unreliable. Memories became distorted, traumatic conditions affected recall, personal biases affected interpretations. Any number of people witnessing the same crime could give differing accounts of what they'd seen. Still, juries seemed to put a lot of stake in them.

"No, they were wearing ski-masks."

"Pity they shot out the damn cameras," Savage muttered. "Was there nothing on the footage?"

"No, the sliver they managed to pull from the CCTV outside the bank showed one man shooting the camera at point blank range. He had a silencer on his weapon."

"A silencer." Savage pondered this for a moment. "I guess they're easy enough to come by."

"Yeah, according to the report, ballistics are trying to trace the make, but it's too general. It won't tell us anything."

"Damn." That would have been a good lead.

Savage wanted to put this case to bed before the baby arrived. Hopefully, they could put Axle and his crew away for the bank robbery, and Candy would be free to live her life without fear.

He said goodbye to Thorpe and hung up.

"Littleton is back today." Barbara beamed as she placed a cup of coffee on Savage's desk. She was fond of the young deputy. "I've baked his favorite apple pie as a Welcome Back present."

Savage's stomach rumbled. He'd skipped breakfast in his rush to get into work, and Barbara's pies were almost as famous as Jasmine Hatch's special brew.

"It'll be great having him back." With Thorpe guarding Candy and Littleton in the hospital, they were two men down. Sinclair had done a fantastic job holding the fort, but she and Barbara needed a break.

He picked up his cup to take a sip when his phone rang. "Savage." He set the mug down again. "What? Where?"

The person on the other end of the line gave him directions.

"I'm on my way."

Barbara scooted out from behind her desk. "What's happening?"

Savage looked up at her. "Marshall Sullivan's body has just been found behind a dumpster at the Sunrise Garden Center. He's been shot in the head."

Her eyes widened. "Oh my gosh. You don't think—"

"Axle didn't like the way he was celebrating his ill-gotten gains,"

Savage murmured grimly. "I'm heading out there now. Tell Sinclair to meet me."

"Can you drive?" Barbara glanced at his bandaged hand. He was still limping from where the bear had mauled him too, but that was healing up well.

At that moment, Sinclair walked in, rubbing her eyes. "Hey guys. Sorry, I overslept." When no one said anything, she looked up. "What did I miss?"

"Marshall's dead," Savage barked.

"What?"

"Last night. Come on." He grabbed his jacket from the back of his chair and shrugged into it.

Sinclair didn't bother taking hers off. "Okay." She pivoted on her toe and followed him out.

"Barbara, can you check those serial numbers for us?" Savage called over his shoulder. "I don't know when we're going to be back."

"Sure thing. Leave it to me." She got up from her desk to go to the evidence locker. "I'll call you once I know."

"What happened?" Sinclair glanced across at Savage as she drove them to the garden center. It was on the road out to Durango, a stone's throw from the Roadhouse. This had Axle's name written all over it.

"I don't know, but I can guess. The garden center manager found his body ten minutes ago when he opened up. The paramedics are on their way, but the guy's dead. His brains are all over the pavement."

She pulled a face.

"There was something else." He glanced across at her. "He was wearing women's clothing."

Sinclair's eyebrows shot up. "You mean—"

"Yeah, it must have happened on his way home from Zeb's last night."

"Oh, crap. We took his clothes." She bit her lip.

"Yeah, poor bastard."

They pulled into the parking lot to see a crowd of onlookers hovering around the body.

"Sheriff's Department," Savage barked, as he strode toward them. "Everybody move back. Out of the way."

Despite getting here as fast as they could, the crime scene was already contaminated. Savage counted five, no, make that six, onlookers, including one with a dog on a leash, sniffing around the body. Beside him, a woman ignored her toddler running in circles around everyone. There were a few snickers and a chuckle as people commented on what the dead guy was wearing.

"Get them out of here," Savage growled at Sinclair.

The crowd began to break up. Sinclair approached the man with the dog. "Sir, if you wouldn't mind removing your pet from the crime scene. You too ma'am. This isn't the place for children."

The woman gave Sinclair a 'whatever' look, grabbed her child's hand, and marched back to their truck. Sinclair rolled her eyes at Savage as if to say, *some people*. She wasn't wrong.

Marshall Sullivan lay on the asphalt, two small bullet holes in his bare chest with a third glistening in his forehead. It looked like the perp had aimed for center mass, and when the biker was down, shot him once more in the head to be sure. Execution style. Whoever shot him meant business.

The spectacular part was what he was wearing.

A woman's fluffy bathrobe, now stained with blood, had fallen open to reveal pink satin panties at least two sizes too small. Savage averted his eyes. That was an image he did not need to see.

"Cover him up," he said, but Sinclair was already on it. Wearing gloves, she took a blanket out of the trunk and laid it over Marshall's dead body, affording him some privacy, even if it was in death. The poor guy didn't need to die with his dignity in pieces, although Savage knew it was too late to worry about that.

The onlookers finally dispersed.

"You the one who found him?" he asked a man in a cheap suit, hovering nearby.

"Yes, sir. Got here to open up the store and there he was, lying next to the trash cans. Scared the pants off me. I've never seen a dead person before." The guy did look kind of pale.

"What time was this?" Savage asked.

"Just after eight. At first, I thought it was a woman, you know. But then—" He didn't need to elaborate. Marshall was a big, hairy guy, and the beard would have given it away.

"We'll need to close the parking lot," Savage told him.

The manager nodded. "For how long?"

"As long as it takes."

"Okay. Sure." Savage could tell he was worried about business.

"We'll be out of your hair as soon as we can," he tried to reassure the man.

A metallic glint caught his eye, and he bent down to inspect two bullet casings. They'd send them to the lab. There might be a history attached to them, but it was a long shot. Axle wouldn't use a registered weapon for an assassination, nor would any of his disciples. They were too experienced for that, and given the accuracy and impact of the shots, this was done by a pro.

"Wasn't Axle in the Gulf War?" Savage asked Sinclair. He seemed to remember someone, maybe Zeb, mentioning that the head of the Crimson Angels had served in Iraq.

"I'm not sure. I'll call Barbara and ask her to pull up his file."

Just then, an ambulance turned into the lot. Savage went over to speak to the paramedics. "The deceased is a Caucasian male. He's been shot three times, twice in the chest, once in the head. No sign of life."

The man gave a stiff nod. "You want us to remove the body?"

"Not yet. I've called the forensic unit. They're on their way."

Sinclair put up a police cordon, and they waited for the CSI unit to arrive from Durango. The unit turned out to be a husband-and-wife team. After making the introductions, they opened the trunk and pulled on full-length forensic suits, shoe coverings, and masks.

"Where are you from?" Savage asked. He hadn't worked with them before.

"Denver," the woman said, smiling. "We came out here to get away from the city."

"It's good to meet you both." He nodded toward the body. "Sorry to call you out to a shooting so early in the morning, but we've got what looks like a professional hit."

"Let's have a look." The woman pulled back the blanket. Neither she nor her husband so much as raised an eyebrow at the dead man's attire, such was their professionalism. Coming from Denver, they'd probably seen it all.

Savage pointed out the casings. "We'll need to get those analyzed."

The woman picked them up using a pair of tweezers and dropped them into an evidence bag. "We'll send them to the lab, but everything has to go to Colorado Springs, so don't expect results any time soon."

That he did know.

"What about the time of death?" Savage asked, even though he could predict it based on the man's clothing.

She lifted his arm and took a look at the underside. Then, laying it back down carefully, she inspected his torso. "The body's almost reached full rigor, so I'd say anytime between ten and midnight."

"You're sure about that?"

"As sure as I can be without doing an autopsy. I'd say this man's been dead for at least eight to ten hours."

Savage thanked her and walked back to the car. "There's nothing more we can do here," he said to Sinclair.

Sinclair nodded. "Back to the station?"

"Nope." Savage pursed his lips. "I think it's time we paid Axle Weston a visit."

THIRTY-TWO

THE ROADHOUSE WAS CLOSED, but two Harley-Davidsons were parked outside, their chrome chassis gleaming in the mid-morning sun.

"Someone's here," Savage murmured, as he and Sinclair approached the bar. It was a wide, flat establishment—not unlike Blake Turner's house—with a row of windows overlooking the parking lot, and a threadbare awning flapping in the breeze. Upstairs, the handful of self-catering rooms were let to the bar staff and anyone else who didn't mind the noise.

Savage pushed the door open, his good hand resting easy on his holster. It creaked, alerting anyone inside to his presence. He didn't think there'd be trouble this time of day, but he wasn't taking any chances. Whoever had shot Marshall was a pro.

Sinclair walked in behind him, her eyes peeled for any sign of movement.

There was a faint smell of stale beer, with an undertone of floor polish. A blues song played on an old-style jukebox in the corner, while a stocky guy in jeans and a black T-shirt lifted chairs off tables and put them on the floor.

The guy didn't look up. "We're closed."

"Morning. Sheriff Dalton Savage and Deputy Sinclair." Savage held out his badge. "And you are?"

The guy stopped what he was doing. "Name's Scooter." He scrutinized the silver star and wrinkled his forehead. "What can I do for you, Sheriff?"

"I'm looking for Axle Weston. I heard he owns this place."

"I'm afraid I don't know who that is."

"Uh-huh." The standard response when anyone came asking for Axle. The man himself was probably watching through a one-way mirror or video camera from a back office. The lie gave Axle time to check out the caller and determine whether he was friend or foe.

Savage looked around. Apart from the barman, the establishment was empty. Two closed doors led out of the main room, one behind the bar counter, and the other on the far side.

"Well, according to the property deed, this place was bought by a Rosalie Weston. I presume that's his wife. I guess we'll just go over to"— He glanced down at the piece of paper he'd pulled out of his pocket— "657 Crestview Drive and talk to her there."

The door at the other end of the room opened and revealed the heavyset man he'd spoken to at Blake Turner's house. Early forties, battle-hardened, rugged. He looked every inch the mean biker in a leather jacket, ripped jeans, and steel-toed boots. The skull dangled around his neck. "Can I help you?"

Savage forced a congenial smile. "Axle Weston. It's good to see you again."

Axle grunted. "Wish I could say the same."

Savage gestured to the deputy. "This is Deputy Sinclair. We'd like to have a word, if you don't mind."

"Actually, I am just in the middle of something. Can it wait?"

"I'm afraid not." Savage's voice was firm.

The President of the Crimson Angels sighed. "Then you'd better take a seat, Sheriff." He gestured to the closest table. "You and your pretty deputy."

Sinclair shot him an annoyed look.

"Can I get you a drink?"

"No, thanks. We're working."

Axle shrugged. "Suit yourself."

The three sat down at the table. Savage leaned back, arms folded loosely across his chest. This wasn't an interrogation, and he wanted Weston to be relaxed. Scooter hovered in the background, never far away. Sergeant in Arms, Savage guessed. Responsible for ensuring the rules of the club were upheld and not violated. A dangerous man. "When did you last see Marshall Sullivan?"

"Marshall. Hmm, let me see." Axle stroked his beard. "Can't have been for a few days now. I think it was last Thursday."

"The same Thursday he was celebrating with his buddy?" Savage glanced at Sinclair. "What was his name again?"

"Walter Minstrel," Sinclair provided.

"Thank you, Deputy. Walter Minstrel."

Axle gave them a hard stare. "If you know, why you askin' me? What's Marshall done now?"

"What makes you think he's done anything?"

Axle arched an eyebrow. "You wouldn't be here otherwise."

"Marshall Sullivan was found dead this morning," Sinclair provided.

Axle's eyes widened. If he hadn't already known about the killing, he was putting on a good show. "Marshall's dead?"

Savage watched the man carefully. "I'm afraid so."

The biker muttered an expletive. "How'd he die? Did he get in an accident?"

It was a common enough question. If Axle hadn't asked, Savage would have been suspicious.

"He was shot. Multiple times." He didn't elaborate.

"Shit, really?" Axle shook his head. He beckoned to the barman. "Get me a drink, Scooter. I think I need one."

Again, very convincing. Sinclair glanced across at him, but he kept his gaze fixed on the biker boss. "Where were you last night between the hours of ten and midnight?"

"Here. Where else would I be?"

"I don't know. Sunrise Garden Center, maybe?"

The older man's eyes narrowed. "Now Sheriff, why would I be there? They ain't open after six o'clock in the evening."

"That's where Marshall's body was discovered."

"Well, I'll be."

Scooter put a finger of whiskey on the table in front of him. Without a word, Axle picked up the drink and downed it in one gulp.

"Can anyone vouch for you?" Sinclair asked.

"Only half the bar," Axle said with a laugh. "I'm afraid we don't have CCTV cameras, ma'am. Our clientele isn't the type to take kindly to being monitored."

"All the more reason they should be," Savage muttered.

"We handle disputes internally." Axle's mouth stretched into a thin line. Behind him, Scooter gave a silent nod. "We don't need no outside help."

"Was Marshall an internal dispute?" Savage asked, looking past Axle to his Sergeant in Arms.

The barman's eyes hardened. Savage noticed a silver scar across his cheekbone as he tilted his face up towards the light.

"No, he was not," Axle replied. "Marshall was a friend."

"You were in the military, weren't you?" Savage asked, his attention back on the biker president.

The question caught Axle off guard. "What of it?"

"Where was it? The Gulf? Afghanistan?"

"The Gulf. Two tours. I don't see what that's got—"

Savage got to his feet. "Thanks for your time, Axle. You don't mind if I call you by your first name, do you?"

Axle shrugged, but it was clear he did mind. The Sheriff wasn't a friend and never would be.

Savage broke into a thin smile. "We'll be in touch if we have any more questions."

Axle gave them a stormy look.

Savage walked towards the door, Sinclair behind him. Before he stepped out into the sunshine, he turned around. "Just so you're aware, we took a wad of cash off your friend and we're having it analyzed. If it matches the loot stolen from the bank in Durango, we'll be back with a search warrant."

A flicker of anger registered in Axle's face. "I don't understand why, Sheriff. What makes you think my club had anything to do with the heist?"

"Call it a hunch. Don't leave town, Axle."

They walked out, leaving the biker president scowling after them.

"WHAT'S NEXT?" Sinclair asked as they got back in the car.

"Let's speak to his wife. He came out of the back as soon as he heard her name. I think she might know something."

"It would be great if we could find that loot," she said. "Can't we get a warrant to search Axle's house?"

"Judge won't allow it." Savage frowned. "Barbara already tried. There's not enough evidence to suggest they were involved. We need more before we bring them in for questioning."

"What about Candy's testimony?"

He shook his head. "Not enough by itself. We'll use her in court when we prosecute. If it gets that far."

Sinclair drove out of the Roadhouse parking lot. "To Durango, then?"

"Yeah. Let's find out what Mrs. Weston knows."

ROSALIE WESTON WAS a striking woman in her early forties with straight, black hair, arching eyebrows over jade-green eyes, and long legs slotted into skinny jeans. Her boots added an extra three inches in height, which put her at eye level with Savage.

"Mrs. Weston?" He held up his badge after she answered the door. "Can we ask you a few questions about your husband?"

She stiffened, thrusting out her chest. "My ex-husband, you mean?"

Somehow, he'd missed that.

"Apologies, I didn't realize."

"That's okay." She tossed her hair back and put her hands on her hips. The woman oozed an angry self-confidence that Savage imagined would appeal to a certain type of man. Hardened biker types, for a start. "What's Axle up to now?" she asked.

"Is he usually up to something?"

She scoffed. "He's a Crimson Angel, ain't he? They're always up to something."

Good point.

"Do you mind if we come in?"

"Sure." Turning her back, she led them across the hallway and into the living room. "Can I get you a drink? Coffee?" She glanced at Savage. "Something stronger?"

"Coffee's fine."

Gesturing for them to sit, she sashayed into the kitchen. Sinclair raised her eyebrows. "She's not what I expected."

"No indeed." He wasn't sure what he had been expecting, but the straight-talking, overtly sexy Mrs. Weston wasn't it.

While Axle's ex-wife was fetching the coffee, Savage took the opportunity to nose around the room. It was sparsely decorated, but with good quality furniture. A comfy leather sofa, a solid oak coffee table, an expensive flat-screen TV mounted to the wall. Nothing recent though. It all looked like it'd been there a while.

Sinclair walked over to a side table. A bunch of gas-station flowers drooped over the side of a wine-red vase. They would have been pretty two days ago. A miniature model Harley Davidson stood next to it, drying petals scattered around. "No photographs.

She was right. There wasn't a single family shot anywhere in the room. No happy wedding day. No young children with chocolate smiles. No family gatherings. Not even a group photo of her time with the Crimson Angels.

"Do you live alone, Mrs. Weston?" Savage asked, when Rosalie came back with a pot of coffee and three mugs on a tray.

She flashed him an emerald smile. "Rosalie, please."

"Rosalie."

"Yeah, ever since I left my old man. The Crimson Angels were my life."

Savage raised an eyebrow.

Rosalie put the tray down and sank onto the couch. "Once you're in the gang, you're part of a brotherhood. A family. That all ended when I walked out on Axle."

"Why did you leave?" Sinclair asked.

Rosalie studied her. "You married, Deputy?"

"No."

"Well, let me tell you something. It's overrated. My ole man, he was cheatin' on me. I gave him an ultimatum, but he wouldn't give her up. So, I left his sorry ass."

Savage exhaled. There was a lot of latent anger there, but also sadness.

"That must have been hard." Sinclair reached for one of the coffee mugs.

Rosalie fixed her gaze on the female deputy. "You've no idea. I didn't just lose my husband that day, I lost everything. In a split second, everything and everyone was gone. Friends I'd known for years didn't want to associate with me anymore."

Savage was content to let Sinclair run with it. The two women seemed to be forming a bond. "I can't imagine what that must be like," Sinclair said.

"I loved my husband," Rosalie said. "But he loved being a Crimson Angel. That life…" She shook her head. "Testosterone, girls, living just this side of the law. He wouldn't give it up."

"You asked him to quit?" Sinclair asked.

"Yeah, I asked him to patch out. Told him we didn't need them, that we had each other. You know what he said?"

Sinclair shook her head.

Savage watched the ex-biker woman's green eyes spark with anger. "He said the Crimson Angels were his family. He refused to leave them." Her voice turned icy. "He chose them over me."

Sinclair grimaced.

"You didn't have any kids?" Savage tried to neutralize the situation. He didn't want Rosalie getting so worked up that she wouldn't talk to them.

It worked. Her shoulders slumped, and she leaned back in her chair. "We weren't so fortunate."

"I'm sorry."

She shrugged. "Wasn't meant to be. The women affiliated with biker gangs are second class citizens. It's a testosterone-filled world. We're supposed to be subservient and obedient, always loyal, never questioning our men, and yet we have to put up with their antics, their cheatin', the rebel lifestyle. To hell with that. I'm glad I'm out."

Savage wasn't entirely sure he believed her.

"I'll get straight to the point, Rosalie. We suspect your ex-husband may have been involved in a bank heist last Thursday. Would you know anything about that?"

She snorted. "I haven't seen Axle in almost a year. How would I know if he robbed a bank?"

Fair enough.

"When was the last time you did see him?"

"Not since I dropped a box of his stuff off at that bar last May." Her voice hardened. "That floozy was there."

"The one he cheated on you with?" Sinclair sounded surprised. "You mean he was still with her?"

"Yeah, that blonde hussy working behind the bar. Wild, feral thing."

Savage felt his heart skip a beat. "You wouldn't happen to know what her name was, would you?"

She frowned. "It was something sickly sweet like Honey. No! Candy. That was it. Candy."

THIRTY-THREE

"YOU WERE SLEEPING WITH AXLE?" Savage yelled, pacing up and down the motel room. "Why didn't you tell us?"

"It wasn't relevant." Candy glanced at Thorpe, who looked devastated. Savage didn't know what was going on between them, but it was something. He could tell by the tension in the air, the way they weren't looking at each other. "That's not why he's coming after me. It's because of what I overheard in the bar."

"Why do I get the feeling there's more to this story?" Savage stared at her, hands on his hips. "Candy, I'm a fair man, but I don't appreciate being lied to. Especially when I'm going out of my way to help you."

Candy dropped her head into her hands. "Okay, I messed up. I'm sorry."

Thorpe had moved away from her and was staring out of the window. Savage gave her a hard look. "I'm listening. Start from the beginning."

She took a deep breath. "They came in around noon, hyped up and laughing. I knew something had gone down, but I didn't know what. Axle was in a good mood, too. He asked for a bottle of Jack, which I took over to their table. They were celebrating."

Savage hung on to her every word. "Go on."

"After a while, Axle wanted to go upstairs. I said I couldn't leave, that we had customers, but he got Monty, one of the other guys, to look after the bar."

Thorpe's shoulders stiffened. "So he wasn't mad at you for overhearing, and you didn't haul ass to the ladies' room?"

She sighed and looked away from Thorpe. Ignoring his question, she continued, "Afterwards, he said everything was gonna change. That he'd come into some money, and we'd go away together, some place nice." She glanced up, her cheeks glistening. "I've never been outside the county before."

Savage gave a sympathetic nod.

Candy swiped at her eyes. "I should have known it was too good to be true."

"What happened next?" Savage asked.

"I asked when, and he said we had to wait a while. That he had a few things to take care of first, but then we'd go. I wasn't allowed to mention it to anyone."

Savage frowned. "What happened? Why'd he come after you?"

"I heard about the bank job in Durango. Everyone was talking about it. I put two and two together and confronted him. I asked him if that's where the money had come from. Said I didn't want any part in a bank robbery."

"What did he say?" Savage leaned forward.

"He asked if I was going to rat him out. I said no, of course not. I just didn't want to be part of it. I wasn't going to tell anyone." Her voice broke. "Then he tried to strangle me."

"He did what?" Savage stared at her.

"He put his hand around my neck and squeezed. I couldn't breathe. I begged him to let me go."

"Did he?"

"No." She shuddered. "I kneed him in the balls and ran."

"What a bastard," Thorpe hissed, reddening. "You should lay an attempted murder charge. Assault at the very least."

She shook her head. "I don't want any more trouble."

Savage thought about what she'd told them. "So you went to Zeb?"

"I didn't know where else to go. He was the one who told me to get out of town for a while. He said he'd send Jesse after me, for protection." This time she did burst into tears. "I didn't know it would turn out like it did. That Jesse…that Jesse would be killed, and that monster would kidnap me."

Thorpe turned around but didn't come near her. "We need to pick up Axle. This has got to be enough to put him away."

"If we can find him." Savage stood up. "I'll get Littleton to come over for Candy. I need you with me."

Thorpe nodded. Savage got the impression he didn't want to hang around Candy, not after her confession. Whatever was happening between them had ended as quick as it had begun. Maybe it was for the best. She was in far deeper than she'd let on.

"You wouldn't happen to know what he did with the money, would you?" Savage asked.

Candy shook her head. "I never saw it. He wouldn't bring it to the bar, anyway. If I had to guess, he'd probably hide it at his ex's place. He's always running off there."

Savage frowned. "She told us she hadn't seen him since last May, when she dumped a box of his stuff off at the bar."

Candy shrugged. "That's not what I heard."

Now that was interesting.

Savage looked at Thorpe. "It seems Rosalie lied to us."

Candy clicked her fingers. "That's her name. Rosalie, except he calls her Rosie."

Savage got to his feet. His body started aching again. "You stay put," he told her. "We'll need your testimony. I'll get ahold of the judge as soon as I can. This might just swing things in our favor and get us an arrest warrant."

Candy looked at Thorpe. "I'm sorry," she whispered.

Thorpe's face was a blank mask. "So am I."

THEY WAITED until Littleton had arrived at the motel before leaving for the station. "What you got there?" Savage asked, opening the door to the young deputy. He was carrying a laptop bag bulging with files, as well as a box that contained Barbara's fantastic apple pie.

"It's a gift from Barbara." Littleton grinned.

"I mean in the bag."

"Oh, this is Axle Weston's military history and rap sheet," Littleton told them. "I thought I'd get up to speed. You never know, there might be something useful." His enthusiasm was admirable.

"We might not need it," Thorpe retorted. His tone was clipped and edgy, and Savage could tell he was still angry about what Candy had told them, or perhaps it was that she'd lied to them. Either way, he wasn't in a great frame of mind. "We've got Axle on attempted murder, and Candy can identify the other two men involved."

Littleton's shoulders slumped.

Savage patted him on the back. He didn't want the young rookie getting demoralized, especially after what he'd been through on the mountain. "It's a good idea and it'll familiarize you with the investigation. If you find anything useful, let me know." Littleton might as well keep himself occupied. It would be good for him to get back to some real police work.

He brightened a little. "Sure thing, boss."

Thorpe drove him back to the station. He didn't say a word the whole way there, preferring to stare out of the windscreen in stony silence. Savage left him alone and leaned back against the headrest and shut his eyes. After this case was over, he was going to sleep for a week.

Barbara jumped up as they walked in, her face flushed. "Guess what?"

Savage felt his pulse surge. "They matched?"

"Yes, Marshall's grubby bank notes matched those from the robbery."

"Axle wouldn't have allowed that." Savage frowned in concentration.

"Marshall must have pocketed some of the loot in the bank, stupid idiot."

"Thought he'd have himself a bit of a celebration," Barbara said. "Except it got him killed."

"That's definitely enough to haul them in."

"I'll get the arrest warrants," Thorpe said. "I've got the names of the other two from Candy's statement. Walter Minstrel and Grady Clemmer."

Savage gave a curt nod. "Then let's hit the road. I don't want to give them any time to escape. They know we've got Candy, so they'll assume she's talked."

"We'll need some help rounding them up," Thorpe said. "They have a small army out there."

"Let's get Durango involved. Maybe even the State Police. Birch might be able to supply some muscle."

"I'll get on it." Thorpe sat down at his desk.

The station buzzed with anticipation. The quiet before the storm. Once they walked into that biker bar with warrants, all hell would break loose. They wouldn't go quietly, Savage knew that much. In addition, the Crimson Angels had some serious firepower.

As soon as the warrants came through, Savage coordinated with the Durango Sheriff's office and the State Police. The plan was to meet at the Garden Center up the road and descend on the Roadhouse, only when they confirmed all three suspects were inside.

Sinclair would be their eyes and ears inside the joint.

"You sure you're comfortable with this?" Savage asked her before they left the station. He didn't want to be condescending, but there would be a lot of testosterone and she might well get some unwanted attention.

"I can handle it. Give me twenty minutes head start, and I'll text you once I see them."

At four-fifteen, while hunkering down in the Suburban behind the Garden Center, Savage received Sinclair's message. "W and G are here. Band leader is nowhere to be found."

Damn.

Savage relayed the info to the other officers waiting with him.

"Let's give it another half an hour," Birch suggested. "If he's not there by then, we'll go in and round up those two. We can't risk them leaving before he arrives."

"He might not even show up," Sheriff Shelby said. "He could be running already or gone underground."

It was a possibility. Savage wanted to give it more time, but the others were impatient. The later it got, the louder it got. The only problem was, if they moved now, they'd lose the chance to arrest Axle. And he was the prize.

"Okay, we'll give it another half an hour."

Time dragged on. Savage kept checking his phone. "Come on," he muttered. "Where the hell are you?"

It was beginning to look like Shelby was right. Axle was on the run.

"The other two might tell us where their boss is hiding out," Thorpe said.

Savage grunted. They might have to play it that way. The President of the Crimson Angels was in the wind with the loot. That was his bet. A man could live for a long time in Mexico on five hundred thousand dollars.

"We're going in," Savage decided, forty minutes later. "Let's round up the others before they disappear, too."

Everyone sprang into action.

Three law enforcement vehicles descended on the Roadhouse and a dozen officers burst in, weapons drawn.

"Everybody put your hands where I can see them," Savage shouted.

After a moment of stunned silence, Scooter and several other bikers stood up, their hands on their holsters.

"Don't do it," shouted Savage. With all these people in here it would turn into a massacre. "Walter and Grady. You know who you are. Nobody else needs to get hurt."

Heads turned, eyes roamed, settling on two men. As luck would have it, they were sitting together at a table with two other club members.

Gotcha, Savage thought. "If you two gentlemen want to come outside with us, we'll have ourselves a chat."

"I don't trust pigs." Grady called out.

"Yeah, me neither," Walter added, spitting on the floor.

The police officers held their weapons ready, waiting for any one of the Crimson Angels to draw. "If you don't come outside with us now, we're going to arrest you." Savage made sure his voice rose above the music. "Can someone turn that off?"

His request went unanswered.

Scooter was getting twitchy. The twelve-gauge on the bar counter was loaded and ready for use. He'd only get off a single shot before one of the officers took him down.

"Don't do it," Savage warned him, locking eyes. "You don't want to die here."

The Sergeant in Arms kept his hands on the shotgun but didn't react. "I think you should get out of my bar." His words were slow, deliberate.

"I'm afraid we can't do that, sir. We have an arrest warrant for your friends here. Either they come with us, or things are going to get messy."

Scooter raised his weapon. Half a dozen guns turned in his direction. Nobody dared breathe.

A male voice said, "Can I make a suggestion?"

Sheriff Shelby had taken a step forward. "Why doesn't everyone else leave?"

There was a collective murmur of approval. Nobody wanted to get involved in a gunfight with the cops.

Savage nodded. "Go, now."

There was a rush for the door. Everyone who wasn't a Crimson Angel left. In the exodus, it was hard to keep tabs on the bikers.

"Stay where you are," Sinclair yelled, her gun to Grady's head. "Don't even think about sneaking out the back."

Savage tutted. "Shall we start again, or do you boys want to get rowdy?"

A few eyes turned to Scooter. It seemed he was in charge when the boss man wasn't around. Savage wondered who the vice president was.

The tension dragged out. Scooter kept his shotgun pointed at Savage. The decision was his, and Savage could tell he was thinking real hard about it.

"Last chance," Savage muttered.

With a sharp exhale, Scooter laid his gun on the bar. Tension drained out of the air. The bikers, taking their cue from him, holstered their weapons or put them down on the tables.

"Hey, what the hell?" Walton groaned.

Savage nodded to Sinclair, who slipped the cuffs on Grady. Shelby did the same to Walton.

SAVAGE CHECKED THE BACK OFFICE, just to be safe. It was deserted. If Axle had been there, he wasn't now. The storeroom behind the bar was also empty.

"Where's your boss?" Savage asked Scooter.

"No idea." Scooter almost spat the words.

Savage wasn't in the mood for attitude. He cuffed Scooter, who protested. "I ain't done nothing wrong. You can't arrest me."

"I can do what I want," Savage said. "That's the beauty of being the Sheriff."

"I ain't involved," he howled, as Savage man-handled him out into the street.

"You can tell that to me in an interrogation room."

They left with the rest of the leather-clad bikers staring daggers at them, but Savage knew they wouldn't challenge him. Not without their president, and it looked like he wasn't coming back.

THIRTY-FOUR

IN THE SQUAD room early the next morning, Savage, Thorpe, Sinclair, and Shelby debated how they would handle the interrogations. They'd left all three suspects to stew in the cells overnight.

"Let's play them off against each other," Shelby suggested, sipping a cup of hot coffee. Savage's respect for Shelby increased the more time they spent together. The Durango Sheriff hadn't said much about his past, other than that he'd spent a long time working for the government before settling down in the neighboring town and running for Sheriff.

Savage nodded in agreement. "I'll take Walton, he'll be the easiest to break."

Shelby grinned. "Be my guest."

"You want me to come along?" Thorpe asked.

Savage grinned. "Nah, this shouldn't take long."

SAVAGE CONFRONTED Walton over the steel table in Interview Room 1. The camera above their heads filmed everything and sent the feed to a computer in the office. The rest of the team would be watching, waiting for Walton to break.

The suspect was a stubborn weasel of a man, with a weak chin disguised by a bushy beard and small button eyes. "I don't know anything about a bank robbery," he whined, when Savage told him what the arrest warrant was for. The big sweat patches under his arms said different.

"There's no point in lying," Savage said. "We know you were involved. Grady already told us."

"He did?"

It was as easy as that.

Outside, he heard a whoop and knew his team was cheering.

"Good job." Shelby congratulated Savage when he came out. "That was one of the quickest confessions I've ever seen."

"He walked right into it." Savage grinned.

Thorpe had gone in to take down a detailed confession. Meanwhile, Grady was waiting in Interview 2.

"My turn," Shelby muttered, and headed for the door.

Grady didn't hold out much longer than his partner in crime. Once Shelby had played him the video footage of Walton spilling his guts, Grady had no choice but to confess. "It wasn't our idea to rob the bank," he told them. "We just did what we were told."

"Whose idea was it?" Shelby asked.

Outside, in the viewing room, the team held their breath.

Savage stared at the screen. *Come on. Say his name.*

Grady's eyes darted from side to side. He licked his lips. Nervous. Beads of sweat appeared on his upper lip. "It was Marshall."

"Marshall?" Shelby narrowed his eyes. "You sure about that?"

"Yeah, I'm sure."

"He's lying." Sinclair threw her hands in the air. "Why would he lie?"

"He's scared. Easier to pin it on the dead guy." Savage strained to hear what Shelby was saying. His voice was low, conspiratorial.

"The thing is, Grady, we heard it was your club president, Axle Weston."

Grady's eyelids flickered. "Nah, man. Axle had nothing to do with it."

Shelby glanced up at the camera and gave a little shrug.

Hell.

Savage turned away in disgust.

"There were four of you in the bank," Shelby insisted, turning his attention back to the suspect. "Who was the fourth man, if not Axle?"

"There weren't four of us. There was only me, Marshall, and Grady."

Shelby loosened his tie. "Eyewitness accounts confirmed there were four bank robbers."

The cameras had been shot out, so they had no video footage of the men entering or robbing the bank. They only had witness statements of terrified bank customers to go by. The defense would argue they were under duress, or that no two witness accounts are ever the same.

"Well, they're wrong."

And so it went on.

"He's not going to break." Shelby came out an hour later. Perspiration dotted his forehead, and he looked weary.

"You tried your best," Savage said, hiding his disappointment. "At least we got two confessions. We can charge these losers while we figure out how to get Axle."

"What about Scooter?" said Thorpe.

"He's tough." Shelby wiped his brow on the back of his sleeve. "He'll never talk."

"He might if he thinks we already know," Savage said. "Walton and Grady could have given up their boss."

Shelby shrugged. "It's worth a shot."

SCOOTER LEANED back in the chair, his arms folded across his chest. He was the antithesis of the anxious, sweaty Walton and Grady. "You can't keep me here. I ain't done nothing wrong."

"You're withholding information," Savage said. "We could arrest you for obstruction of justice."

"What information?" The suspect stared blankly at Savage. It was a good act, but he wasn't buying.

"Information about your boss, and the bank job last Thursday."

"What?" The barman threw back his head and laughed. "You're crazy."

"We know he was there," Savage said casually. "Walton and Grady confirmed it."

There was a flash of uncertainty, but then it was gone.

"Nice try, Sheriff." Scooter smirked. "If those two clowns robbed a bank, then that's on them. I don't know anything about it. I can tell you, however, that Axle was at the Roadhouse all afternoon. We went through the takings for the month."

Savage ground his teeth.

"What do you know about Marshall Sullivan?"

"Marshall?" Scooter's face clouded over. "He was a good guy, but I heard he got involved in some strange shit. He was gunned down and left in a dumpster wearing women's clothing." He shook his head. "In all the years I've known him, I never thought he was that way inclined."

"Why would someone do that, do you think?" Savage asked. "Gun him down."

"Heck, how the hell should I know? Ask the chick whose clothes he was wearing."

"He had a girlfriend?"

"Not that I know of."

Savage sighed. This was going nowhere. Shelby was right. Scooter wouldn't talk, not for anything. He was loyal to Axle and quite happy to let Walton and Grady take the fall for the bank robbery. Hell, as soon as he got out of here, he'd probably update Axle on what had happened. Savage made a mental note to put a tail on him.

"Let him go," he told Thorpe when he got back to the squad room. He looked at Shelby. "You got a spare deputy to tail Scooter?"

"You think he might lead us to Axle?"

Savage shrugged. "You never know."

Shelby tilted his head. "I'll see what I can do."

"Thanks."

"Axle's gonna keep gunning for Candy." Thorpe's voice was strained, and worry lines were etched into the corners of his eyes. "She's the only person who can prove he was involved. His crew's not ratting him out."

"They're too afraid of what he might do to them," Savage muttered.

"Ironic, since the bastard doesn't give a flying you-know-what about them. He's in the wind with the loot, and their cut."

"Fear is a powerful motivator," Sinclair said.

She wasn't wrong there.

Shelby got off the phone. "Birch and his team set up roadblocks at the county line, but it feels like shutting the barn door after the horse already bolted."

"You think we'll ever find him?" Sinclair asked.

"I hope so," said Thorpe dismally. "Otherwise, Candy's never going to be free of him."

Savage sighed. It wasn't looking good. "Maybe it's time I put in that call to WITSEC."

Walton and Grady were charged with bank robbery and would have their day in court. With their own confessions backed up by Candy's testimony, they'd get four to six years. In the meantime, they put out a BOLO on Axle Weston, in the event that he showed up.

"Maybe we should try his ex-wife's place again," Savage suggested. It was mid-morning and another beautiful spring day. "I have a feeling she held back last time we spoke to her."

"You think he's hiding out there?" asked Thorpe.

"I don't know. It's a possibility, considering what Candy told us."

"Okay, I'll get the car."

They were about to leave when Savage's phone rang. It was the Somers Institute in Pagosa Springs. He listened for a moment, heart slamming against his chest. "No, she left around eight this morning. She should be there by now."

Everybody stopped what they were doing and turned towards Savage. His voice was hollow. "Thanks for letting me know. Please get her to call me if she comes in."

"What's happened?" Sinclair asked, the second he hung up. "You look like you've seen a ghost."

Savage gripped the desk as an icy chill swept over him. "Becca didn't make it into work today."

THIRTY-FIVE

NOT BECCA.

Savage stared out the car window as Thorpe floored it towards the Somers Institute in Pagosa Springs. Fear clutched his chest, making it difficult to breathe. Closing his eyes, he forced himself to think logically, calmly. She could be running late. Maybe she stopped to pick up some baby supplies. There could be a reasonable explanation as to why she hadn't gotten to work yet.

Except, he knew. Even as these scenarios flew through his brain, he knew. A sharp pain, like nothing he'd ever felt before.

Breathe. Don't lose it. Stay calm.

Perhaps she'd broken down, or had a minor accident? There had been no traffic accident reports, but maybe she was stranded on the side of the road, waiting for the breakdown service.

He tried her cellphone again. It diverted to voicemail.

Savage wasn't a religious man, but he found himself praying.

Please let her be alright.

Panic threatened to rise, choking him. He clasped his hands together tightly, the knuckles white. "If anything happens to her—" He couldn't even finish the sentence. Dread like he'd never known before flooded his body, consuming him. His mind went blank. A white haze of pain, like the static on a faulty television screen.

"We'll find her." Thorpe murmured, his hands stiff on the steering wheel. He didn't take his eyes off the road.

The highway sliced through the national forest as they sped along, the tall trees on either side whizzing past in a hazy blur. On either side of the road was a deep ditch, man-made, to prevent animals from running into the traffic—although that still happened.

Savage kept his eyes peeled for any sign she'd run off the road. Skid marks, grease stains, rubber fragments from a burst tire. But he found none.

It was a forty-minute drive to the institute, most of it on the highway. They were almost at the midpoint when Savage pointed to the side of the road. "There!"

Thorpe slammed his foot on the brake and swerved onto the shoulder. Luckily, no one was behind them. Traffic on this stretch was thin until the post-work rush.

Skid marks. Cutting through the vegetation on the side of the road, disappearing over the edge into the deep trench. Beyond that, the forest stretched for miles, dense and inaccessible.

No. No.

Before Thorpe had a chance to park, Savage jumped out of the SUV and ran to the edge. He could see where a vehicle had flattened the bushes in its frantic trajectory over the embankment.

Was it her?

Becca's blue Toyota.

"It's her car," Savage rasped.

Thorpe, running up behind him, was almost as pale as he was. "I'll call 911."

Savage didn't think before sliding down the muddy slope and stumbling through the bushes towards the vehicle. Trunk open, metal crumpled, steam hissing out from the hood. How long had she been here? Was she even inside? Was she alive?

"Becca!" Savage yelled, stumbling the last few feet. He looked for positives, desperate for some hope, even just a flicker. The car was mostly intact, except for the hood buried in dirt, and its nose creased up like an accordion. That would have been quite an impact. The airbags would have activated.

"Becca!"

There was no answer.

Had she swerved to avoid an animal? A deer maybe?

He knew. He just didn't want to think about it.

There was no reply.

"Becca, are you in there?" Savage peered through the cracked side window. Becca's dark head was crumpled forward on the steering wheel.

"She's still in there," he barked.

Thorpe had scrambled down beside him. "Ambulance is on its way."

The door wouldn't open. Gripping the handle with both hands, he heaved, but it didn't budge.

"It's buckled from the impact. Let's try the other one." Thorpe moved around to the other side of the vehicle, Savage on his tail. Together, they gripped the door and pulled it open. It creaked and groaned, but they forced it back wide enough to get in.

"Becca, can you hear me?"

A faint moan. His heart surged. That was all he needed. She was alive.

"Becca, we're here. We're going to get you out."

She managed to raise her head off the steering wheel and turn it to the side. "Dalton? Is that you?"

"It's me, sweetheart. I'm going to get you out."

The airbag had activated on impact and was now a partially deflated pillow between her stomach and the bottom of the steering wheel.

"Thorpe, help me." Savage dove into the passenger seat and unbuckled Becca. There would be a red welt across her chest where the belt had dug in, maybe a cracked rib or two, but it had probably saved her life.

"What happened?" she murmured.

"You had an accident, but you're going to be okay." He prayed she was.

Her head lolled back against his arm.

Thorpe reached in to help.

"Easy," Savage breathed as they maneuvered her out of the door. He didn't want to make her condition worse, and he couldn't tell how badly injured she was. There was a nasty gash on her head, and blood was smudged against her cheek, but it looked like the airbag had done its job.

They got her out of the wreckage and laid her gently on the ground. Savage stroked her face, and she stirred, her eyelids fluttering.

She tried to lift her head. "The baby—"

"Don't move," Savage told her, laying her head back on the ground. "Wait for the ambulance to get here."

"—Connor?"

"Everything looks fine." He put a hand on her stomach. "The airbag deployed, so everything's going to be fine." He didn't want to distress her any more than necessary. She needed to get checked out by a medical professional, and soon.

"Are you in pain?" Thorpe asked.

"My head—" She winced. "I hit my head."

"You may have a concussion," Savage said. "We'll get you checked out soon."

Where the hell was the ambulance?

Becca gasped and tried to sit up. "I was driven off the road." She gazed up at Savage, her eyes wide and unfocused. "I remember now. He bumped into me from behind and forced me off the road." She squeezed her eyes shut as a spasm of pain hit her.

"Who? Who bumped into you?"

"A gray car. I think it was a Chevy."

Savage gritted his teeth. He knew just who that was. "Did you get a look at the man?" he rasped.

"Yeah. Forties, dark hair, gray beard. Looked like one of those biker types."

Savage met Thorpe's gaze.

Axle Weston.

The President of the Crimson Angels had tried to injure his fiancé. He was sending Savage a message.

Stay away or else.

THE AMBULANCE HAD TAKEN Becca to the emergency department at Mountain View Medical Center in Pagosa Springs, the nearest big hospital.

Savage shot up from his seat as the doctor entered the waiting room.

"The baby's fine," Dr. Palmer said. Savage had been sitting in the waiting room, mainlining black coffee for the last few hours. "The airbag saved her."

Thank God. A wave of relief turned his legs to mush. He put a hand on the wall to stabilize himself.

"That's great news, and how is Becca?"

"Your wife was lucky. She's got a concussion, but there's no bleeding on the brain. She was unconscious for a few hours, but the CAT scan didn't show anything abnormal. I have no doubt she'll make a full recovery."

"Thank goodness." Savage didn't bother to correct him. Wife sounded good. "Thanks, doc." He pumped the man's hand. The anxiety he'd been carrying began to dissipate.

"Can I see her?"

"Sure, she's conscious, if a little groggy." He smiled at Savage before moving off down the hallway.

"Becca, I'm so sorry," were the first words out of Savage's mouth as he strode into the ward. Becca was propped up against the pillows, a band-aid on her forehead where she'd hit the steering wheel, and an eye turned a deep shade of purple.

She held out her arms, and he fell into them, hugging her as hard as he dared. "This is all my fault."

"None of it's your fault," she murmured.

He extricated himself and gazed at her face, bruised but beautiful. "If it wasn't for this case, that bastard wouldn't have come after you."

"You didn't know," she whispered, although there was worry in her eyes. "You couldn't have known."

"I should have known. I should have been more careful." He'd provoked Axle. It was a stupid thing to do. He'd never had to think about anybody else before. Now he had a fiancé and a child on the way. People who mattered to him.

"You don't think he'll try again, do you?"

His voice was hard. "I won't give him the chance."

She gripped his hand. "Don't do anything rash, Dalton."

"I don't want you to worry about him. I'm going to take care of it."

She gave a stiff nod and squeezed his hand. "Promise you'll be careful. I don't want this baby growing up without a daddy."

"I promise." He scowled, his eyes narrowing. "Axle's running scared. He knows we've got him. That's why he's panicking."

"Is this the man who robbed the bank?"

"Yeah, him and his crew. We picked up the other two yesterday, but they won't rat out their boss. They're too scared of him."

"What about Candy?" Becca lay back against the pillow. "Is she safe?"

"As safe as she can be under the circumstances." He took a deep breath. "As soon as Axle's put away, she'll be a lot safer."

"That poor girl." Becca shook her head. "To think that Axle's the reason she headed up into the mountains to begin with."

Savage perched at the end of the bed. "It's been a crazy week. We get one whack job to let another on the loose."

"You look tired," she said softly.

"I'll rest when this is over." Savage clenched his jaw. "When Axle's behind bars."

"How are you going to find him?"

"The state police set up roadblocks. Unless he's on foot, he can't get out of the county. It's more likely he's holed up somewhere with the loot, waiting for things to die down."

She stared up at him, her face almost as pale as the pillow under her head. "He could be anywhere."

"Don't worry." Savage smiled grimly. "I've got a plan."

THIRTY-SIX

"YOU CAN'T USE her as bait." Thorpe looked horrified. "What if he kills her?"

"It won't come to that. We'll make sure of it." Savage's face was a determined mask.

"I don't like it." Sinclair shook her head. "It's too dangerous."

They were at the station, having an impromptu meeting in Savage's office. Barbara had pinned an A4 photograph of Axle Weston to the wall, a visual reminder of the man they were hunting. The fugitive stared down at them, his flat eyes mocking, his lips pulled back in a permanent smirk. Savage looked forward to putting a line through it. "Besides, how will we leak her location to him? He's in the wind."

Savage sat down. "His ex, Rosalie."

Sinclair stared at him. "I don't understand. They don't speak."

Barbara pursed her lips and said, "That's sneaky, Dalton."

"It's the only way."

Sinclair and Thorpe exchanged looks.

"What are we missing?" Sinclair asked.

"Rosalie hates Candy," Savage explained. "She's the blonde hussy responsible for her husband's infidelity. If we let slip where we're keeping Candy, I guarantee you Rosalie will tell Axle."

"But Rosalie doesn't know where he is," Thorpe reminded them.

"They keep in touch. Candy suggested he might have even hidden the loot at her place. She'll know where he is, or at least she'll know how to find out."

Barbara's eyes lit up. "She used to ride with that crew. Scooter will know where he is, and I'm betting he'll tell her."

"A woman scorned and all that." Sinclair shot Savage an admiring look. "Good plan."

Thorpe sighed. "I guess it's worth a shot. If Candy agrees."

"She won't have a choice." Savage was firm. "If she wants a new life, she'll do this for us. It benefits her if we put him away, almost as much as it does us."

Barbara raised an eyebrow. "I can see this is important to you."

"Axle Weston is going down," he gritted. "One way or another."

———

WHEN SAVAGE ARRIVED, he found Rosalie sitting on the porch, a glass of bourbon in her hand. He'd come alone, figured it was better that way. More believable.

She didn't get up. "Hello again, Sheriff."

"Good evening, ma'am." He walked up the stairs and stood in front of her.

"You gonna join me?"

"Do you mind?"

"No, I'm glad of the company. You still working, or can I tempt you with a real drink?" She tilted her glass.

He hesitated. "Why not? I'll have a small one."

She broke into a smile. "Now that's the spirit."

He took a seat in the rocking chair beside hers. It was a mild evening, the sun setting over the mountains, painting the valley in a peachy hue. The distant mountain peaks had turned purple in the dusk.

Rosalie disappeared inside, then reemerged with another tumbler.

"Great view," he said, looking out.

"Yeah, I like it out here. You can see for miles, all the way to the mountains. It makes you aware of your own insignificance." The whiskey tinkled as she poured it into his glass.

"It does that."

She handed it to him. "Is this about Axle again? Because I already told you, I don't know where he is."

The way it rolled off her tongue, the woman was good. He'd never know she was lying. He decided to play her game. "I know, but I thought you could give me some ideas. You know him better than anyone."

"Knew," she pointed out. "It's been a while."

Savage shrugged and took a swig of the drink. It warmed him up as it went down. "Still better than nothing. We think he's going to go after Candy, the girl you told us about. The one he was in a relationship with. They're still together, by the way. He told her about the money he stole from the bank. Promised her they'd run away together. Thing is, Candy didn't want anything to do with it."

Rosalie's lips tightened. "Why are you telling me this? I don't know where the girl is?"

"That's okay. We've got her somewhere safe, but we can't let her go until Axle's behind bars. Do you think you can help us out?"

Rosalie gazed at him, saying nothing. He let the silence drag out, taking another sip, giving her time to think about it.

Eventually, she clicked her tongue. "I wish I could help you, Sheriff, but like I said, I don't know where he is."

"But you could find out."

Her eyes narrowed into jade-green slits. "You want me to go asking around? I told you, none of the Crimson Angels talk to me anymore. I'm an outcast, a citizen. I don't belong."

Savage shrugged. "Someone must know where he is. Say you've come to warn him. Tell him I came to see you."

"Now, why would I do that?"

"Because you still have feelings for him. Hell, I don't know. You think of something."

She made slow circular movements with the glass, watching the amber liquid swirl round. "You want me to rat out my own husband?"

"Ex-husband, right?"

She shook her head. "I know he did me wrong, Sheriff, but I'm not a snitch."

Savage looked at her for a long moment, then threw back the rest of the drink and got to his feet. "In that case, Rosalie, there's nothing more for us to discuss."

"DID SHE BUY IT?" Sinclair asked when he got back to the station.

"I think so. My bet is they'll start following us to find Candy."

"And we'll lead them straight to her?" Thorpe still wasn't happy.

Savage cocked his head. "That's the plan."

"I don't like it."

"You don't have to like it." Savage locked eyes with his deputy. "It's still a good plan, and it's the only one we have. I'm not going to risk him going after Becca again."

Nobody commented.

"Okay." Sinclair took a deep breath. "When do you want to do this?"

"Let's give her a day or two to get ahold of Scooter. Thorpe, you sit on her, but make sure she doesn't make you. We may as well tell Shelby to call off his deputy." They didn't want Scooter getting suspicious.

Thorpe gave a stiff nod.

"What do you want me to do?" Sinclair asked.

"We're going to talk about what happens once he finds her."

SAVAGE SPENT the next few days with Becca, who'd been released from the hospital. He took her home and stationed a deputy from the Durango Sheriff's office outside the house, just to be safe. With Littleton guarding Candy, Sinclair in the office, and Thorpe shadowing

Rosalie, they didn't have the manpower to offer any form of protection.

He didn't think Axle would try again. The car wreck had been a warning, and the biker boss wouldn't risk coming out of hiding. Not for that.

But he might for Candy.

On the second day, Thorpe called. "Rosalie made contact. Just walked into the Roadhouse."

"Who's she talking to?"

"Scooter."

Savage allowed himself a small smile. "Good."

It was time to implement the second part of their plan.

———

LITTLETON LEFT the Sheriff's office early the next morning and drove to a convenience store. He bought sanitary pads, deodorant, and other feminine products. He took his time, inspecting the various items, checking the labels.

Thorpe, sitting in an unmarked van outside, spoke rapidly into his phone. "One of Axle's crew just followed Littleton inside."

On the other end of the line, Savage replied, "Good. We have action."

Littleton emerged from the store, glanced left and right, then climbed into his car, putting the shopping bag on the passenger seat beside him. He wasn't using a squad car for obvious reasons, and even though he wore his deputy's badge, it was hidden underneath his jacket.

"Remind me never to recommend Littleton for undercover work," Thorpe said. "He's terrible at it."

Savage gave a snort. "That's the idea."

Thorpe watched as the young deputy pulled out of the parking lot and drove off. The biker followed at a discrete distance. Not obvious enough to arouse suspicion. Thorpe followed the biker, his phone on speaker. "He's on his way."

"Roger that."

Thorpe exhaled. It was happening as Savage had predicted. He only hoped it wouldn't go to hell in a handbasket once they got to the motel. Candy didn't deserve to die. She'd been through enough. First that psycho in the mountains and now this. How much bad luck could one person have?

Thorpe's gut wrenched. An image of her wild hair and laughing eyes flashed through his brain, but he shook his head, refusing to go there. She'd been sleeping with Axle. She'd lied to them. To him. He couldn't come back from that. The sooner she was placed in witness protection, the better.

Tensing his jaw, he followed the biker, weaving in and out of the mid-morning traffic. Hawk's Landing wasn't a big town, but this was the busiest time of day. A truck pulled in front of him and he lost sight of the motorcyclist for a second.

It didn't matter. He knew where the biker was headed. The motel was only a few blocks away, at the quiet end of town.

Littleton pulled into the motel parking lot and got out of his car, the brown paper bag under his arm. He looked around as if to make sure he hadn't been followed, then proceeded up the stairs to the motel room.

The sun glared down on the dirty white exterior of the building, making Thorpe squint. The biker had his visor down, so his features were hidden, but it wasn't Axle's build. This was a messenger sent to report back to the president on Candy's location.

As expected, the motorcyclist watched until Littleton knocked on door number seven and disappeared inside. Then he turned around and drove off.

Thorpe picked up his phone. "We're in play."

THIRTY-SEVEN

LITTLETON LEFT the motel room a little before eight o'clock. The sun had sunk behind the mountain range, turning the sky indigo. There was no breeze. The scent of pine and fir trees hung in the air. A wood fire burned in the distance.

"I'll be right back," he called. "Make sure you lock this door."

A blonde head poked out. "Okay, hurry back."

He walked along the external walkway and down the stairs to the parking lot, then climbed into his unmarked vehicle and took off.

Across the street, Sheriff Shelby called Savage. "He's gone. No movement from the white van."

A cable repair van had been parked outside the motel for several hours, but nobody had gotten in or out. It could have been a guest, staying in one of the motel rooms, or it could have been a surveillance van, reporting any activity back to Axle Weston and his crew. Savage was betting on the latter.

They'd run the plates and gotten a hit. Registered to an address in Durango.

"Let us know if anything changes," Savage replied.

Savage, Thorpe, and two deputies from Shelby's team sat in the adjoining motel room to Candy's. Blinds down, lights off. Only a dim flicker from the bathroom prevented it from being pitch dark. From the outside, the room appeared empty.

"Are you sure they'll come?" Deputy Montgomery asked. Monty, as he was known by his friends, was a big guy, six foot five, and he spent a lot of time in the gym.

"I'm not sure about anything." Savage shot him an annoyed glance. "But she's alone in the room. If they're going to strike, they'll do it now."

There was no CCTV at the motel. This was Hawk's Landing, after all.

"Makes sense," Deputy Dickson replied. He was the pacifier, soft-spoken with eyes that didn't miss much.

"They're my best men," Shelby had promised. "They'll get the job done." Savage hoped Shelby was right. He didn't want any screw ups.

"Axle can't afford to let her live." Thorpe's voice was a hoarse whisper.

The time ticked on. Outside, dusk faded into night. It had been a half hour since Littleton had left. If the thugs were coming, they were leaving it very late.

Savage sighed. Perhaps he'd been wrong. Maybe this was all for nothing and Axle wasn't going to fall for his sting operation.

Monty checked his weapon, the clicking grating on Savage's nerves. Dickson sat mute, shoulders relaxed, feet together, not moving a muscle. Everything about him screamed military. Savage was betting sniper.

"Come on," Savage murmured. "Where are they?"

Thorpe fixed his eyes on the laptop, showing a video feed from Candy's room. They'd installed a small camera above the bed to capture anything. Juries tended to sway towards photographic evidence, and Savage wasn't taking any chances.

The radio crackled and Shelby's voice came on. "We have a visitor. A silver Ford Taurus just drove in. I can't make out the occupants yet."

"Keep us posted." Savage's heart skipped a beat. Could this be them?

Monty flexed his hands, while Thorpe wiped his palms on his trousers. Dickson didn't move.

Savage got up and stood by the door. He couldn't risk taking a peek in case they had a camera focused on the motel. The slightest movement from a blind, a shadow at the window, or a sliver of light from inside would send a signal to the bikers, who had a well-honed sense of criminal paranoia. This was his one shot at getting Axle and his gang. He wasn't about to blow it.

Shelby crackled through the phone again. "We have movement in the parking lot."

They waited. Nobody spoke. Savage held his breath.

"It's them," came the excited response. "I repeat, it's them. *Axl Rose* and two band members are getting out of the vehicle. All three are armed. I repeat, they're armed." Turns out Shelby was a rock 'n roll fan.

"Roger that." Savage exhaled. "What about the surveillance van?"

"Nothing yet."

Strange, he could have sworn one of Axle's guys was in there.

"Hang on. Van door's opening." They heard an exclamation. "We have another band member. That's four in total. All armed."

Shelby was right. The guy in the van had been watching the motel all day, waiting for the right moment to strike. As soon as Littleton had left, he'd placed a call to his boss.

Showtime.

Savage looked around. "Ready?"

They'd been over the plan several times. Everybody knew what to do. The deputies nodded, shoulders tense, faces somber. Savage knocked three times on the wall and then drew his gun. Thorpe and the two other deputies did the same.

They got into position. Monty and Thorpe at the front door, Savage and Dickson at the adjoining door. It was a two-sided assault. Divide and conquer.

Timing was everything. A woman's life depended on it.

"They're walking up the stairs," Shelby's voice, giving them a running commentary. He was their eyes and ears outside the motel. "They're on the walkway now. Almost there. A few more steps. Bingo."

They heard a splintering thud as one of the thugs kicked in the motel door, followed by a volley of muted bangs. All eyes flew to the in-room camera. Two shooters, both using suppressors. And one of them was Axle Weston.

Yes!

"We got him," Savage murmured. Thank goodness the bikers hadn't thought to cover their faces. Arrogantly, the gang assumed they'd be in and out in seconds.

The other two men stood guard in the walkway, guns at the ready. They were backup. With that kind of firepower, Candy wouldn't have stood a chance.

The deputies looked at Savage for their cue. "Now!"

Monty swung open the motel door and stepped into the walkway, surprising the two bikers. "Police! Drop your weapons!" He gave them a chance to comply. Instead, they opened fire, startling a pigeon who took flight above them.

Monty darted back into the room as the bullets sprayed the door frame. The gunshots echoed down the narrow walkway.

So that's the way this was going to play out. They should've known the biker crew wouldn't go quietly. It wasn't in their nature.

Savage nodded to Dickson, who pulled open the adjoining door. Axle and his sidekick had their backs turned, distracted by the firefight outside.

A guttural yell told him Monty hit one of the gun thugs. There was a heavy thud as the man went down.

Thorpe raised his gun. "Put your hands in the air. Now!"

In a heartbeat, Savage crossed the room. "Freeze, asshole." Axle spun around to find himself staring at the steely business end of Savage's service pistol. He took one look at the expression on Savage's face and slowly raised his hands in the air.

His sidekick twisted around, finger on the trigger.

"I wouldn't." Dickson rested his gun against the man's temple.

Outnumbered and outgunned, the thugs gave up.

Shelby appeared on the walkway, out of breath. He'd raced across the road after hearing the gunfire.

"Please don't shoot," Axle begged, handing his weapon to Shelby.

Savage took Axle's pistol and clicked on the cuffs. Dickson did the same to his sidekick.

"One fatality," Monty called in the walkway.

"You're under arrest for attempted murder," Savage informed them.

"Attempted?" Axle frowned and glanced back at the bed. It was riddled with bullets. The pillow had been reduced to wool, and all that was visible beneath the bedspread was a mop of fake blond hair.

"Sinclair?" Savage called.

Sinclair walked out of the bathroom. "I'm here." She was wearing a blond wig.

Axle stared at her. "Hey, you're not—"

"Surprise." She took off the wig, shaking out her dark hair.

Axle groaned.

Thorpe walked into the room and stared at the pock-marked bed. "Jesus. It's a good thing we got her out of here." Not taking the chance, they'd moved Candy to a more secure location earlier in the day. Littleton was with her now.

Sinclair had been hiding in the bathroom in case the shooter realized it was a sting and checked the bed. As it turned out, they hadn't suspected a thing.

Not only did they have Axle Weston for attempted murder, but also for the bank job. Even if he didn't admit to killing Marshall Sullivan, he was going away for a long time.

More importantly, Becca was safe.

THIRTY-EIGHT

"IT'S DONE," Savage told Becca when he got home. "We got him."

It was late, but she was still up, waiting for him.

Axle and the two thugs had been booked and would spend the night in a jail cell at the Hawk's Landing Sheriff's office. Tomorrow, they'd be transported to a county jail to await trials. As for the man Monty had shot, his body had been taken to the morgue. There'd be a lengthy report to fill out on the shooting, but since the thug had fired first, he didn't anticipate a problem.

"He had no choice." Shelby had told Savage afterwards.

Choice or not, it was still a big deal taking a man's life. Monty would have to undergo obligatory counseling, and his firearm would be taken away from him until the investigation was concluded and it was deemed a 'good' shooting.

"You mean we're safe?" Becca put her hand on her bump.

Savage stared at it. Hard to believe that was his son in there. A surge of protectiveness washed over him. "Yes. You're both safe."

She grasped his hand. "Thank you, Dalton."

Weariness spread over him. It had been a long day. A long week.

"Come to bed," she said, but Savage didn't move.

"In a minute."

He was still processing. The setup, the waiting, the shoot-out, the arrest. It could have gone so differently. Luckily, none of his and Shelby's team had been injured.

Becca shifted. "You okay?"

"I am now."

"Do you want to talk?"

"No, not right now." All he wanted to do was enjoy the peace and quiet of his own home, the feel of Becca's hand in his, and her presence next to him.

Words could wait.

She nodded. "Maybe tomorrow then. You know I'm here, right?"

"I know. That's what makes it okay."

"What about Candy?" she asked. "Is she safe now?"

"Not yet. Axle could send someone after her. Once the trial's over and he's sentenced, things should settle down."

He didn't mention Rosalie. Her plan to get rid of Candy hadn't worked. What would she do now? Would she try again? Or let it slide? Now that her ex was in prison, was it worth the effort?

"When's the trial?" Becca asked.

"Not sure yet. Could be six months or so, I'd guess."

"You'll have to keep her safe until then."

"I know. That's easier said than done in Hawk's Landing. Now the motel's been compromised, we'll have to find a new location."

"How about out of town?" Becca suggested. "Somewhere like Pagosa Springs."

Savage stared at her. "You know what? That's a great idea."

She looked pleased.

"We can hide her at the institute."

"At the Somers Institute?" Her forehead wrinkled.

"Yeah, why not? It's perfect. Several displaced kids live there. It's got round the clock supervision. She'd be safe there."

"Those kids suffer from mental health challenges," she reminded him. "They're under constant monitoring."

"Even better. Candy would benefit from being part of the program. She's been through a hell of an ordeal. We can hide her there until she testifies."

Becca sat up in bed. "I'm not putting my patients at risk, Dalton. What if someone comes for her?"

"They won't. Nobody will know she's there. It's the perfect hiding place. Besides, it's only temporary. Once she testifies, we won't have to worry anymore."

She sighed. "I suppose it could work."

Savage leaned over and kissed her. "Thank you. You're doing a good thing."

"I hope I'm not going to regret this."

"It'll be fine. I promise."

After a long, hot shower, Savage crawled into bed beside his fiancé. She was asleep, her chest moving up and down in a steady rhythm, but she murmured when he put his arm around her.

This. This was why he'd done it. For his family.

Still, it was a long time before he finally drifted off to sleep.

"LET ME GET THIS STRAIGHT," Savage exclaimed a few days later. "Rosalie Weston is now head of the Crimson Angels?"

The team was at the station, crowding around Savage's desk. Sinclair had just walked in with a huge flask of Jasmine's special brew and was pouring it into polystyrene cups. The scent of roasted coffee beans filled the air.

"Yeah." Shelby had dropped by on an unofficial visit to give them the news. "She waltzed into the Roadhouse a couple days ago and made an announcement. Her name is on the deed too, and now that her ex is out of the picture, she's the sole owner."

Savage shook his head. "That's one crafty woman."

"You think she ratted him out to get control of the MC gang?" Sinclair stopped what she was doing and glanced up.

Savage arched an eyebrow. "She must have. I thought she was doing it to get rid of Candy, but I was wrong." Rosalie had played them at their own game.

"They must know she snitched," Thorpe said.

"Hard to prove, though," Savage replied. "Scooter was the only person who knew, so if he's still there, his loyalty is obviously to her."

"He's still there," Shelby confirmed with a firm nod.

"The King is dead. Long live the Queen," Barbara murmured, coming out from behind her desk to grab a cup.

Thorpe's shoulders sagged. "This is bad. Candy's never going to be safe. Not with that woman gunning for her."

Savage gave a sage nod. "I think you're right. It looks like we're going to have to put her into WITSEC after all. She can't stay here in Hawk's Landing."

"Poor kid," Barbara said. "How's she doing, anyway?"

Only their team knew where she'd been placed. Not even Shelby had been privy to that.

"As well as can be expected. It'll be good to see her settled somewhere permanent. She's been through a lot."

"You got a trial date yet?" Shelby asked.

"Yeah, early next month. Not long to go."

"We're getting our paperwork in order," Thorpe added. "We had some good news about the bullet casings."

"Which bullet casings?" Shelby asked.

"The ones found on a shooting victim a couple days ago. We know it was Axle and his crew, but we couldn't prove it."

"We can now." Thorpe's eyes sparkled behind his glasses.

"Oh yeah?" Savage arched his eyebrows.

"Ballistics couldn't match the casings with anything on the system, but..." Thorpe grinned, "Axle Weston's fingerprint was on one of them."

"No way." Savage couldn't believe their luck. "It must be from when he loaded the gun."

"Yeah, which gives us concrete proof that he murdered Marshall

Sullivan," Thorpe added. "He may deny pulling the trigger, but he loaded the gun, which is close enough."

"We know he put the hit out on him," Sinclair said. "And we know he was in the military, so it makes sense that he killed him that way."

Shelby exhaled, raising his coffee cup. "Here's to catching the bad guys. Rumor has it, you took down a nasty serial killer too."

"That we did." Savage inclined his head.

"Impressive."

They raised their cups and everyone took a welcome gulp of coffee.

"Damn, this is good." Shelby glanced at his cup.

Savage smiled. "Well done, team." He looked at each of them.

"Here's to more collaboration in the future," Shelby said. "I can see we're not done with the Crimson Angels yet. It's a brand-new ballgame with Rosalie in charge."

Savage nodded. "I was afraid of that."

"Still, let's enjoy this little victory, shall we?" Barbara cut in. "Before we start thinking about the next one."

She was right. The next case would come along soon enough.

SAVAGE MET Candy on a bench in the garden at the Somers Institute. The green lawn had recently been cut and the smell of fresh grass permeated the air. In the background, the modern psychiatric building spread out over the lawn as if stretching in the morning sun.

It was a lovely spring day, blue sky, no clouds.

Perfect for a new beginning.

"How are you feeling?" he asked her.

"Nervous." She wrapped her arms around herself. She looked skinnier than before. "I've never left the county before. Barely left Hawk's Landing."

"I know it's a big step, but you're a strong woman. You'll be okay."

Her lip trembled. Right now, she looked more like an anxious teenager than an adult. "I hope so."

He smiled. "I know you will. Look at everything you've been through. Compared to that, this will be a walk in the park."

Her eyes got some of their sparkle back.

"You'll get a new identity, a new place to live, a new life. Nobody will know where you are. You'll be safe again."

She exhaled under her breath. "That sounds wonderful." Then her face clouded over. "Are you sure he won't find me?"

"I'm sure. As long as you follow the rules and don't contact anyone from Hawk's Landing, you'll be okay."

"Don't have anyone to tell. Not anymore."

He gave a solemn nod. She wasn't close to her mother, hadn't even asked about her, and now Jesse was dead. She had no one else.

Savage got to his feet. "Well, this is goodbye. Take care of yourself, Candy."

After a moment's hesitation, he held out his hand, but she ignored it and threw her arms around his neck. "Thank you, for everything. If it wasn't for you coming after me in those mountains. And again with Axle." She shook her head. "I don't know what I would have done."

"You're welcome." Just the mention of the mountains was enough to make his hand twinge. It was healing slowly, the bones starting to knit together, but was still tender.

She released him and moved away. The WITSEC agent waited to take her to a facility where she'd be briefed, processed, and transported to her new life.

"Take care, Candy."

"Um, Sheriff?"

"Yeah?" He turned around.

"Does it ever get any easier? Living with the memories, I mean."

He hesitated. He thought about the men he'd killed. The shooter he'd taken out in Denver—his first. About the others along the way.

Did it get easier? No, not really. Every one of them was a memory, a face he carried around in his head. But he couldn't say that to her. She deserved a fresh start.

"It does," he said. "You'll get there."

She broke into a grin. "Thanks. That means a lot."

Savage turned around and kept walking. Someday he'd have to confront his past. If not now, then soon. There was one memory he had to put to bed before it ate him up inside. But that was a task for another day.

Right now, he was going home. To his family.

***

Dalton Savage returns early 2023 in **Scorched Earth**! Click the link below to pre-order your copy now!
https://www.amazon.com/dp/B0BLCVKJ5Y

Join the L.T. Ryan reader family & receive a free copy of the Rachel Hatch story, *Fractured*. Click the link below to get started:
https://ltryan.com/rachel-hatch-newsletter-signup-1

ALSO BY L.T. RYAN

Click on a series name or title for more information

The Jack Noble Series

The Recruit (free)

The First Deception (Prequel 1)

Noble Beginnings

A Deadly Distance

Ripple Effect (Bear Logan)

Thin Line

Noble Intentions

When Dead in Greece

Noble Retribution

Noble Betrayal

Never Go Home

Beyond Betrayal (Clarissa Abbot)

Noble Judgment

Never Cry Mercy

Deadline

End Game

Noble Ultimatum

Noble Legend (2022)

Bear Logan Series

Ripple Effect

Blowback

Take Down

Deep State

Rachel Hatch Series

Drift

Downburst

Fever Burn

Smoke Signal

Firewalk

Whitewater

Aftershock

Whirlwind

Tsunami

Fastrope (coming 2023)

Mitch Tanner Series

The Depth of Darkness

Into The Darkness

Deliver Us From Darkness

Book 4 (2023)

Cassie Quinn Series

Path of Bones

Whisper of Bones

Symphony of Bones

Etched in Shadow

Concealed in Shadow

Betrayed in Shadow

Born from Ashes

Blake Brier Series

Unmasked

Unleashed

Uncharted

Drawpoint

Contrail

Detachment

Affliction Z Series

Affliction Z: Patient Zero

Affliction Z: Abandoned Hope

Affliction Z: Descended in Blood

Affliction Z : Fractured Part 1

ABOUT THE AUTHOR

L.T. Ryan is a *USA Today* and international bestselling author. The new age of publishing offered L.T. the opportunity to blend his passions for creating, marketing, and technology to reach audiences with his popular Jack Noble series.

Living in central Virginia with his wife, the youngest of his three daughters, and their three dogs, L.T. enjoys staring out his window at the trees and mountains while he should be writing, as well as reading, hiking, running, and playing with gadgets. See what he's up to at http://ltryan.com.

Social Medial Links:

- Facebook (L.T. Ryan): https://www.facebook.com/LTRyanAuthor

- Facebook (Jack Noble Page): https://www.facebook.com/JackNobleBooks/

- Twitter: https://twitter.com/LTRyanWrites

- Goodreads: http://www.goodreads.com/author/show/6151659.L_T_Ryan

Printed in Poland
by Amazon Fulfillment
Poland Sp. z o.o., Wrocław
28 February 2023

a7586eb9-6767-4cf4-b0db-82b5de001bf2R01